ALSO BY MICHAEL NEWTON

Gideon Thorn

Skinwalker

Leviathan Rising

Ghost Town

Mountain Devils

SOUL SLAYERS

SOUL SLAYERS

GIDEON THORN
BOOK 5

MICHAEL NEWTON

Soul Slayers
Paperback Edition

Dark Wolf Books
An Imprint of Wolfpack Publishing
1707 E. Diana Street
Tampa, FL 33610

www.darkwolfbooks.com

Paperback ISBN 979-8-89567-909-8
Ebook ISBN 979-8-89567-908-1

Dedicated to Michael Pate, the first movie monster of the new Old West.
(1920-2008)

SOUL SLAYERS

PROLOGUE

MAY 18, 1876: SAN DIEGO COUNTY, CALIFORNIA

"Your parents know you're out here, Enzo?" Randall Drummond asked, and then repeated it in Spanish. "*Sus padres saben que estás aquí?*"

Standing beside him, head-high to his hip, Enzo Velasquez answered, "*Sí, Señor.*"

"You sure about that," Drummond pressed him. "Let's go ask, just to be sure."

"No, *por favor!*" the almost nine-year-old responded hastily. "I mean, no need to bother them, *Jefe*. They like it when I help you, learning things about the *rancho.*"

"Yeah, that's what I thought," Drummond allowed. "Come on, then. But if they get angry at you—*enojado, comprender?*—you can't be using me as an excuse."

Smiling to beat the band, Enzo replied, "*Nunca, Señor. Lo juro.*"

"No, don't swear. Just make sure it's the last time you come sneaking out right after supper."

"*Sí. Usted tiene mi palabra.*"

"Well, your word will have to do," said Drummond, smiling now himself. "Just one man to another."

"*Dos hombres,*" the youngster parroted, his chest puffed out with pride. "What are we doing, then?"

"Checking around the place as usual, to make sure everything's secure. You know about coyotes getting at the chickens?"

"*Sí,*" Enzo replied, his dark eyes wide with outrage. "*Es muy malo.*"

"Damn right it's very bad," the rancher said, then caught himself. "Don't tell your ma you heard me cussing, right?"

"*Es nuestro secreto,*" the child assured him, white teeth bright by early moonlight.

"Yep. Our secret. That's the ticket, *hombre.*"

They were moving toward the barn now, fifty yards or so from Drummond's ranch house where he lived alone. He was a widower, had no children that he knew of anywhere, and even at a youthful forty-some years old, he'd started thinking about who would get the ranch when he was gone.

Not for a while yet, sure. But still... Things happened on a ranch that no one could foresee, and one mistake could be a person's last. His wife proved that, dying in childbirth twelve years past, and their infant son days later, even though a doctor and a wet nurse tried their best to save him.

Anything could happen, and it would someday. Drummond harbored no fantasies of immortality, but if he found a woman somehow, somewhere, who could love him or pretend to—

"*Qué fue eso, Jefe?*" Enzo's tense voice cut through his thoughts.

"I heard it, too," Drummond acknowledged. "Sounds like something's in the barn besides our stock."

"*Los coyotes malditos!*"

"Best not let your *madre* hear you cussing, much less blame the cause of it on me."

"No, no, *Jefe*. What will you do? Go back and fetch your rifle?"

Drummond thought about it for a second, but it meant another round trip to and from the house, while God knew what was happening inside his barn, to animals that mattered for the ranch. Besides, he had the Colt revolver on his hip, and that would deal with any predators too dumb to run for it when he surprised them.

"No time now," he told Enzo. "You'd best wait here until I see what's going on."

Reluctantly, the small boy answered, "*Sí, Señor*" and watched while Drummond started moving toward the dark but not so silent barn.

Enzo Velasquez waited all of ten seconds before he followed in the rancher's wake.

Around behind the Drummond farmhouse, fifty yards due west, Sofia Velasquez completed the last of her nightly chores before bed and wiped her hands on a threadbare dishtowel. The small house—four rooms, situated on a square floor plan—was once again as clean as she could make it without learning *brujeria,* and she put no stock in witches' magic, anyway. Her husband, Mateo, worked long days for Mister Drummond on the ranch, and Enzo, bless his scheming heart, found new ways of distressing her each day. It made her think about the life growing inside her, where the second child would sleep, and how her work load would be more than doubled with another mouth to feed.

But there was nothing to be done about it now. *Jesucristo* dispensed his blessings as it pleased him, never thinking of the inconvenience they might cause to mere mortals.

Putting the towel away, Sofia had to smile, thinking that she and sweet Mateo weren't exactly innocent in this case, either. He seemed happy at the news of an impending second child, coming sometime in October or November, but Sofia also saw the worry lines around his eyes and mouth when they sat down in rare free moments to consider baby names.

As if in answer to her thoughts, Mateo stepped into the kitchen, asking, "Where is Enzo?"

Frowning at the question, she replied, "In bed, I hope."

"Then you must hope for something else. His blanket is turned down, but I can't find him anywhere."

"*Ese pequeño diablo,*" she half-whispered through clenched teeth. "And did you check his window?"

"Shut, not latched," Mateo said.

"He's off pestering *Señor* Drummond yet again." Sofia felt the angry color rising in her cheeks. "I've told him three times, now."

"And twice from me," Mateo said. "*Voy a tener que pegarle ahora.*"

Despite her anger, word of an impending spanking gave Sofia pause. "Must you, Mateo? We both know he idolizes *Señor* Drummond, how he loves to help, as he calls it, around the *rancho.*"

"*El jefe no es su familia,*" Mateo answered back, confirming what they both already knew. The widowed boss was not a part of Enzo's family.

"Perhaps if we both talk to him together," she suggested.

"I'll consider it," Mateo said, no more excited by the thought of paddling his only son than was Sofia. "But I have to find him first, and then apologize once more to *Señor* Drummond for the inconvenience."

"I think he likes Enzo," Sofia said.

"It makes no difference. We lay down rules for Enzo's safety, and to keep our jobs. Suppose he makes *el jefe* angry and he sends us packing?"

"He wouldn't do that," she protested. "Not over a child who worships him."

"And that's another thing," Mateo said. "It is *blasfemia* to worship, as you say, a man instead of *Dios.*"

"I did not mean—"

Mateo's tone softened. "I know what you meant, *mí corazon.* But he must still obey his parents, and before we find a way to drive that message home, I have to track him down. Again."

Trying to scowl, if not convincingly, Mateo left their house to go in search of Enzo one more time.

Standing resolute in darkness, breathing in the smell of cared-for animals, their feed and waste products, Gabor the predator turned toward the darkened barn's west wall and flared his nostrils, straining to reach past the odors that surrounded him. Hushed voices, of a man and child, had reached his ears and warned Gabor that it was nearly time to act.

Another step toward the completion of his mission and the victory he craved.

"*Ahal,*" he warned the others, in the old tongue, barely whispering. It meant "wake up," although Gabor knew none of them were sleeping, risking sudden death from negligence. The lone word cautioned them to be ready for action without further warning, hewing to the plan he had devised, the plan that they would carry out on pain of death and worse.

Now footsteps were approaching, drawing closer to the barn but without the expected urgency. Their target—the adult—was wily and on guard, ready to fight after their prior visits to his property had helped him see a threat he understood, which would not overtax his lowly *tso'o'nom*—his brain.

The target came prepared for danger of a sort, but one he was accustomed to, had already defeated countless times over a span of years on land he thought of as his own. He believed that a *ch'amak* had trespassed on his property and stolen birds he claimed like all else he controlled, through arrogance and foolish pride.

The target was about to learn a lesson and, at the same time, provide a service to his betters. Gabor cared nothing about the child who tagged along with his intended prey. Whether this *paal* survived the night or not depended absolutely on his courage at a tender age.

Gabor could kill him or allow him to survive. It made no difference to him either way.

Now he could feel the man, as well as smelling him and hearing him. He read the adversary like a scroll laid bare, convinced that he would neither run away nor call for reinforcements from the bunkhouse where his ranch hands spent their nights after a long day's work.

The prey would enter any moment now, with or without the boy.

His fate was sealed.

Gabor edged closer, silently, and felt the stealthy shadows follow him.

The sounds, whatever Randall Drummond thought he'd heard inside the barn, had ceased. He had two choices now: shrug off the incident, dismissing it as his imagination, or continue on and satisfy himself that nothing was in place to tamper with his stock.

And even as that thought formed in his mind, he knew there was in fact no choice.

He *had* heard something, whether it was some invasive predator, merely a rat, or even just a stray night wind, what Enzo and his family would call *viento de la noche*. It was Drummond's job, his calling, to protect his property and rule the spacious ranch he'd built from nothing, battling nature, Indians, and border trash to stake his lasting claim.

Even if it were just a rodent scuttling through the barn, making the horses shy and whinny, he would face it down and deal with it. Plus, he could not afford to let young Enzo think he had been spooked, even if something made the short hairs on his nape bristle.

Drummond decided not to draw his Colt as he was opening the barn's broad door, fighting its drag against the dry earth of the farmyard. He needed two hands for the door, just then, and also didn't want Enzo to think that he was showing off—or worse, brandishing iron because he was afraid to step inside his own damned barn at night.

Ridiculous.

He wasn't some child frightened of the dark or anything that might be hiding in it.

So, get on with it, a small voice in his head suggested. *Stop this wasting time.*

Drummond knew where to find a lanten, hanging just inside the barn's door for a situation such as this one, when his stock were troubled after dark. His first bold stride across the threshold helped, made him feel more self-assured, then he was turning to his right and reaching out to find the lantern that he couldn't really see just yet.

He felt his fingers graze the lamp's glass chimney and was following it toward the brass hook up above, when suddenly the sound of running footsteps and a strange, unearthly *rustling* noise came at him from behind.

Swallowing a cry of sudden panic, Drummond fumbled for his Colt.

Mateo Velasquez was scanning the farmyard for Enzo, preparing in his mind how he would scold the boy this time, when he was startled by a pistol shot. Although Mateo owned no guns himself, he'd been around enough of them to recognize the sound and differentiate it from a shotgun blast or rifle's whiplash crack. He froze in place, then swiveled toward the barn, convinced the shot had come from there.

What now?

Clearly, he could not rush into a killing situation empty-handed. But did he require a weapon now?

Most likely, *Señor* Drummond had discovered a coyote in or near the barn, one of the prairie scavengers he'd been complaining of the past few days. Whether he'd killed the beast or not, only a fool would run into his line of fire without some verbal warning to alert him first.

And one thing no one ever called Mateo was a fool.

Behind him, in the doorway to his humble home, he heard Sofia calling out, "Mateo, *que esta pasando?*"

How in hell would *he* know what was happening, without investigating further? Turning toward the spill of light that framed his wife, hissing at her, "*Silencio! Volver a entrar!*"

She glared at him, letting Mateo know they would discuss his giving orders later, but then did as she was told, stepping back through the doorway, closing it behind her, shutting out the night.

Mateo turned back toward the barn and called out in its general direction, angered by the tremor in his voice, "*Jefe!* Is everything all right?"

No answer from the boss, and no more gunfire in the night. Whether the single shot was good or bad, Mateo couldn't guess.

He tried again, louder this time. "*Señor* Drummond! Can you hear me?"

Others were stirring in the bunkhouse now, the *jefe*'s half a dozen other hands roused by the shot. They milled about in lamplight, jabbering, too far away for Mateo to catch their words.

A sudden image flashed into his mind of Enzo, wandering around the ranch without permission after nightfall, and Mateo flushed with shame at his forgetfulness. The boss had still not answered him, but now Mateo shouted for his son. "Enzo! *Dónde estás? Ven a mi!*"

A high-pitched squeal came from the open doorway of the barn then, and Mateo's son came running toward him, stumbling once and falling, bouncing back again from outstretched hands, his wailing incoherent as he ran into his father's arms. Sofia joined them seconds later, drawn by

Enzo's screaming to ignore Mateo's strict command. Both of them clutched the weeping boy and peppered him with questions.

"Where is *Señor* Drummond? Who was shooting? What is happening?"

Enzo pulled back from them, his small face streaked with tears of fright. When he began to speak at last, his jumbled words seemed senseless to Mateo and Sofia.

"*Las aves gigantes! Tomaron el jefe. El se fue.*"

Mateo shook the boy, and none too gently, ordering him to repeat what he had said.

"The giant birds!" his son repeated. "They took him! He's gone!"

ONE

MAY 20, 1876: MOUNT CHARLESTON, NEVADA

Gideon Thorn breathed in the mountain air, urging his stallion forward on the winding uphill track. Nine thousand feet below him and thirty-five miles behind, to the northwest, the tiny village of Las Vegas faded into misty desert distance, no more than a handful of homes surrounding an old Mormon fort built as a trading post in 1855, with just enough inhabitants to rate a flyspeck on most maps.

Thorn knew Las Vegas meant "the meadows" in English, but now he was getting a taste of the Nevada's translated name. It meant "snow-capped," a nod to the mountains that surrounded the mostly-desert lowlands in between, and Mount Charleston was one of the tallest, looming nearly twelve thousand feet over the Spring Mountains range that separated Nevada from southern California. Evergreens and other trees flanked Thorn's rising trail, and there was still some gritty snow underfoot, even at this time in May.

Thorn had taken his time riding out from Las Vegas, spending two nights in the open, last night at the very foot of Mount Charleston. He didn't worry that the creature he was hunting might detect his fire and flee before he scaled the peak. Possessed by monumental arrogance, a sense that he could get away with doing anything that crossed his mind, Thorn's prey would not uproot himself from someplace he regarded as safe ground.

That very arrogance, with any luck, would be the end of him today.

The creature, as Thorn thought of him, was christened Isham Reed Winslow a few days after birth in Kansas, raised by parents who feared God so much and took His word so literally that they never missed a chance to beat their offspring for the least infraction, whether actual or just a figment of their warped imaginations. They had made a monster of him, through no fault of Isham's own—but he was still a monster, nonetheless, and was responsible for every brutal thing he'd done as an adult during the past twenty-odd years.

A part of that was breaking from his parents' church, which troubled Thorn no more than a divorce obtained by anyone shackled to an abusive mate. Although he wore the emblems of various faiths on a silver chain around his neck—a Star of David, a crescent for Islam, a cross for Christianity, a mandala blending Buddhism and Hinduism, a pagan pentagram and a feather representing America's native tribes—Thorn cared nothing for any particular dogma. People, in his view, might use religion as a guide, a crutch, even a weapon, when they lacked ability to deal with life head-on.

In Isham Winslow's case, fanatic fundamentalism had induced rebellion from an early age. From what Thorn knew, his crimes had started small, fire-setting, torturing small animals, stealing and lying for the hell of it. Within the past few years, however, he'd evolved, choosing a path that set him on a hard collision course with the faith of his parents.

Over the past two years, to Thorn's certain knowledge, Winslow had kidnapped seven young girls from various towns across Utah Territory and Nevada, savagely abusing each in turn but leaving them alive—after he'd branded each in turn with an inverted cross upon her back, stomach —or, in the latest outrage, on her face.

One of the victims had already purged her pain and shame through suicide. The rest had been sequestered by their "loving Christian" families or else packed off, either to live with distant relatives or, in one case, to finish off her childhood in an orphanage. Thorn had collected details of the crimes from neighbors, relatives, the odd lawman—and from a jailed accomplice of the predator, who'd named his "master" for a Utah lawman.

Not that it had helped to run him down. That took a special kind of tracker, one who worked outside the law when it encumbered him.

Gideon Thorn was not a bounty hunter in the common sense. He had no need for monetary payoffs when he solved a case and brought a perpetrator—human, animal, or otherwise—to something that approximated justice. Solving an enigma was its own reward, even if he regretted it in hindsight, wishing that he could forget what he had learned.

A smell of wood smoke brought his senses into focus. Moments later, he picked out the rough, slumped outline of a cabin set well back among the trees.

Could it be the place he sought? How many squatters

lived upon Mount Charleston, overlooking the Nevada desert from its heights? Thorn knew that there was only one way to find out.

Winslow's last victim had been snatched from Pioche, near the Utah border, and recovered wandering, delirious, by silver miners south of town. Plotting Winslow's crimes on a map, Thorn had discerned the monster's drift from northeast to southwest, and hoped to stop him before he claimed any further innocents.

If that meant stopping Winslow dead, Thorn reckoned he was fine with that.

And afterward, another mystery was waiting for him farther west, in California.

Thorn came prepared for anything that might confront him in the mountain wilderness. He wore twin Colt Peacemakers on his hips, and his saddle boot held a Winchester Model 1873 chambered for the same .44-40 cartridge as his two pistols. His Sharps Model 1872 in .50-90 caliber, mounted with a special telescopic sight, rode aboard his pack mule, but he didn't count on needing it for distance in his present situation. If the action moved *too* close, he also had a twelve-inch Bowie sheathed behind his back, together with a shorter dagger that protruded from the high top of his right-hand boot.

Now all Thorn needed was a target he could recognize from the description and distorted sketch on Isham Winslow's WANTED poster out of Utah Territory.

Reining in Shadow, his gray stallion, Thorn dismounted and removed his lever-action rifle from its scabbard. Keeping silent, he sent calming thoughts out to his horse and mule, a talent he'd discovered during early childhood, still not fully understood but useful in a pinch with species that included certain mammals, birds, and reptiles.

As for humans...well, he had to deal with them by other means.

Checking his Winchester unnecessarily, to satisfy himself it had a cartridge in its chamber, Thorn had covered half a dozen yards uphill to reach the solitary cabin when a gruff voice from his left announced, "That's fer enough, Mister."

If Isham Winslow thought about it, living like a hunted animal had its advantages. He'd always felt like an outsider, from the first time that his parents beat the living hell out of him for some paltry "sin" he couldn't even understand. It wasn't long before he had accepted torture as his due, convinced the only proper course of action for a boy "born bad" must be to follow through and take advantage of his nature, grateful for the lack of conscience life had handed him.

And since the grim religion of his forebears labeled him a waste of life, what better way to celebrate his difference than by accepting Satan as his savior, signing on the dotted line in blood. Of course, it wouldn't be *his* blood, if Winslow had his say.

And so far, since he'd run away from home, no one had laid a finger on him yet.

Not that they hadn't tried. And now, here was another one.

The latest tracker didn't fit the mold Winslow was used to. In the past, he'd dealt with old, pot-bellied lawmen and their posses made of nervous shopkeepers who spooked and ran as soon as someone started shooting at them. Once, a rangy killer had come after him, looking like someone who had spent the summer hunting grizzlies in a mountain range somewhere, but he had proved unfit for hauling in a human animal.

This one was... different.

For starters, he was damned well dressed, decked out in black from his flat-brimmed hat to his high-topped boots, all except for the white shirt beneath his frock coat. He wore twin revolvers and carried a Winchester '73 that Winslow coveted on sight, a good piece to replace his Henry lever-action if it ever let him down.

Above all, the hunter was *young,* mid-twenties at the most. Winslow thought he must be six foot four, at least, and likely tipped the scales around 180 pounds. Youth should've made him easy to dispose of, but from hiding, Winslow had to say that there was something older in the hunter's shifting eyes.

It might be something dangerous.

So Isham took him by surprise, watching him ease in closer to the cabin he'd found empty, two weeks back, and called out to him through the trees, "That's fer enough, Mister."

"You're pretty good at that," the tracker said, eyes homing on the sound of Winslow's voice and pinning him.

"I'm good enough to get the jump on you. Now set that rifle down."

The man in black obeyed, and Winslow stepped into the open, holding steady with his Henry as he closed the gap between them, step by cautious step. "Don't try'n reach them pistols," he instructed, "or I'll shoot ya in the gut and let ya die real slow."

"More mercy than you showed the children, anyway."

"So that's what brung ya here." Smiling as best he could —a facial twist someone had told him once could curdle milk—Winslow eased closer, stopping when about six paces lay between him and the enemy. "I taught 'em somethin', didn't I? They'll grow up wiser women, 'cause a me."

"Jane Elkins won't," the tracker said. "You might've heard she killed herself."

"One weak un in the bunch so far. It could be worse."

"Worse for the ones that lived, maybe. If you can call it living."

"Kids're tough," Winslow replied. "Just lookit me."

"I'm looking."

As the stranger answered him, a rustling in the pine to Winslow's right distracted him. He shot a glance in that direction, never deviating with the Henry's aim, and felt himself relaxing as he recognized the great horned owl.

Winslow rasped out a laugh and said, "Looks like a hootie come to watch you die."

Thorn hadn't tried to call the owl, or any other bird specifically. That portion of his mind worked on its own, sometimes, taking advantage of the landscape and its fauna in a useful but subconscious way. He'd hoped for a distraction, but now thought he might have stumbled onto something even better.

Winslow, startled by the owl's arrival, had relaxed without a hitch and got the twisted smile back on his face. "Nice of you bringin' up all kinds a presents for me," he remarked. "It feels like Christmas Day come early."

"Happy to oblige," Thorn said.

"I bet you is," the ravager replied. "I like yer horse, expecially. Might have to eat the mule, but you won't mind, I guess."

"Looks like you're holding all the cards," Thorn said.

"Damn straight." Winslow was gloating now, full of himself, but something seemed to nag at him. "Guess ya got somethin' that ya wanna ask me, first?"

"Like what?" Thorn countered, buying time, his eyes shifting to find the owl's and making contact there.

" 'Like what,' he says," the monster fairly spat back, mocking thorn. "Same thing they all asks, dammit! How'd I get this way? What made me how I am? How can I live with what I done?"

"I know all that," Thorn said, shifting his gaze back from the great horned owl to Winslow's disappointed-looking face.

"Ya think so?" Winslow challenged him. "Whyn't ya prove it, then?"

"I know about your parents," Thorn replied. "I have a fair idea of what you went through as a kid. It warped you somehow, deep inside. You steal the innocence of others now, because your own was stolen from you by the folks who should've loved and sheltered you. You hate the world and set yourself apart from it in every way you can."

"You sound like one a them head doctors, sayin' I can still come back and have a useful life."

"If someone told you that," Thorn said, "I wouldn't trust his word on anything."

It wiped the last trace of the crooked smile from Winslow's face, replaced by a flush rising from the collar of his filthy shirt into his cheeks. "You'd call me hopeless, then?"

"From the first minute when you laid hands on a child."

"Bodes ill for you, I guess."

"Not necessarily."

When he communed with animals, Thorn didn't try to

frame his thoughts in words. None of the wild creatures he'd met spoke English, so he would've been wasting his time. What worked for him, most times, was feelings, sent along with images of what he hoped a given animal might do or, in a pinch, refrain from doing. Making contact wasn't all that hard, but to communicate sensations and impel action was something else again.

It was a gamble, then, but Thorn was ready when the great horned owl launched from its perch, screeching a *ke-yah, ke-yah* cry it might have borrowed from a nighthawk, and sank half-inch talons into Winslow's face, beating its two-foot wings about his head as if in a demented frenzy.

Thorn was ready when the Henry rifle cracked and sent a .44 slug through the space he'd occupied a fraction of a second earlier. He'd started moving when the owl did, hopping to his left and whipping out his right-hand Colt and cocking it before he sent a silent break-off message to the screeching bird. The owl flapped up, up, and away as Winslow tried to strike it with his Henry's barrel, missing by a foot or more.

While he was cursing, flailing at the empty air, Thorn shot him in the back.

It wasn't how a gentleman might get it done, but Thorn was far past caring.

And it worked.

The slug knocked Winslow sprawling facedown on a bed of last fall's leaves and pine needles, the rifle tumbling from his grasp and out of reach. Thorn moved to stop him reaching any hidden weapons he might have, using a toe and leverage to roll the wounded man onto his back. The way his legs dragged on the roll, Thorn guessed the bullet must have clipped his spine.

"It isn't looking good for Christmas," he advised.

"That goddamn owl," Winslow wheezed up at him.

"How'd ya pull that?"

"You wouldn't get it," Thorn replied. "Besides, you're done."

"Notice ya couldn't face me like a man." There was a sneer on Winslow's face and in his tone.

"I wasn't dealing with a man," Thorn said.

"Somethin' about ya." Winslow had begun to gasp now, running out of breath. "Can't put my finger on it."

"There's no point in trying."

"You don't aim to take me in?"

Thorn slipped his pistol back into its holster. Said, "You wouldn't make it down the mountain, much less back to Pioche. Anyway, I have another job to do."

Already looking westward, to the California border, the Mojave Desert, and what lay beyond.

"So, you'll just leave me here?"

"Like you did with the girls. Or you can pull a hideout gun after I'm gone and speed things up."

"Suppose I get healed up instead, and then come lookin' for ya?"

"No," Thorn said. "Your legs are gone. You're bleeding out. I'd give you ten or fifteen minutes, tops."

"I curse you, then," Winslow replied. "You didn't know I had that power, did ya?"

"I'll just have to take my chances," Thorn replied, backing away and out of range, to where his animals were tied.

He'd mounted up and was already passing Winslow's cabin, knowing that the quickest way around Mount Charleston was straight over it and down the other side, when he heard Winslow calling after him.

"Curse you!" the fading voice echoed. "Damn you to Hell!"

"I guess we'll see," Thorn muttered to himself, then concentrated on the ride ahead of him.

Once he had cleared the mountain, it was still another twenty-odd miles to the California border, plus two hundred miles approximately to his destination. Call it another two weeks on the trail without harming his animals, and if the mystery was solved before he got there, Thorn would call it someone else's turn to find good luck.

But something told him it would still be waiting, maybe even having gotten worse while he was on the road.

It was a chance he'd have to take.

TWO

MAY 22, 1876: BOSTON, MASSACHUSETTS

It was safe to say that Jared Connor didn't love his job. Some days he hated it, in fact, when friends he'd known from school saw him around the city, pedaling his bicycle the way he had back then, but now with telegrams inside the basket on his handlebars, delivering the latest news no differently than when he'd been a paperboy at twelve years old.

The problem was that time had passed. Connor was nineteen now, and all his former friends had found their places in the world, whether they manned cash registers in shops downtown or had gone on to what the bluebloods liked to call a higher education. Jared, for his part, had dropped out of school after his father died, to work and help his family in South Boston, and he could feel his former classmates looking down on him whenever chance brought them together on the street, almost as if they longed to whip diplomas from their pockets, laughing while they waved the goddamned papers in his face.

But here he was, almost a man under the law, no better off to speak of than he'd been at fifteen, when the liquor took his old man and he'd given up on any dream he'd ever had of finding fame and fortune in his life.

Sometimes it was enough to make you hate the world. Most days, Connor refined his brooding rage to focus on a given nationality that seemed intent on crowding decent Irish out of Beantown, treating those who'd come before them as if they were worthless placeholders, just waiting to be shoved aside.

Connor could still remember signs he'd seen in various shop windows, growing up, that read NO DOGS OR IRISH NEED APPLY. That attitude was still apparent throughout much of Boston, though his countrymen had infiltrated politics all right and had a stranglehold on the police department now. Connor himself had thought about joining the cops, but he'd been sickly from the time he'd learned to walk and wasn't fit to swing a club at lesser immigrants, apparently.

So, screw 'em. He'd keep cycling through the streets, delivering the good and bad news to his Western Union customers and cursing them under his breath, behind their backs.

Like now, pedaling hard to make the climb up Beacon Hill. Only the wealthiest of all Bostonians lived in proximity to the Massachusetts State House, in the one square mile of mansions north of Boston Common and the Boston Public Garden, centered on the Shawmut Peninsula and bounded on the west by the Charles River's mouth on Boston Harbor. Climbing the hill itself always reminded Connor of his status in society, a bottom-feeder marked for menial employment from the miserable day when he was born.

Today's first stop on Beacon Hill took him to Pinckney

Street, near Louisburg Square. Connor recalled from school that the square had been named for some battle he could never keep straight in his head, between the French and what became Americans after the War of Independence. Locals basked in pride about it, all the more reason for Connor to forget it and move on.

The address he was seeking fit a grand four-story pile that loomed above the tree-lined street like someone's vision of a castle built in olden times. Connor knew before he stopped his bike and started up the flight of marble steps that he'd be dealing with a snotty butler wearing a black morning coat, black tie, gray vest and gray striped trousers, with shoes polished so highly they could serve as mirrors for the old fart peering down his nose at any working man who came to call.

"Just get it over with," he muttered to himself, and started up the steps. A stout brass knocker fashioned in the likeness of a lion's head, the cat gripping a large ring in its mouth, echoed inside the palace when he lifted it and let it fall back into place.

And then, of course, he had to wait, because that's what the rich folks and their lackeys made a common worker do. Their time was worth a fortune, while nobody else's mattered in the least. Connor resigned himself to standing there, feeling a fool, then he was startled when the massive door swung open without any sound of footprints drawing near to let him brace himself, draw back his shoulders, and put on a smile he didn't feel.

But that wasn't the half of it.

The stocky butler staring down at him this time was wearing tailored tweed instead of the traditional attire, his barrel chest and biceps straining at the seams of his jacket. He didn't smile, which was the norm, but rather eyeballed Connor as if he were perfectly unique, a curiosity.

Strangest of all, the man who towered over him was black.

Obi Magoro eyed the white man poised below him on the mansion's steps. He wore a Western Union cap and an ill-fitting jacket to match, over a threadbare white shirt and trousers that could stand a pressing. His shoes were brown and cracked across the top, their dull finish suggesting it was weeks since they had met a polish rag.

The visitor had red hair sticking out from underneath his cap in all directions, rarely combed from its appearance. Freckles marked cheeks flushed as if the day were cold instead of seasonably warm for Beacon Hill. Green eyes had gaped at Obi when he first opened the door, but now they'd narrowed with a look that mixed suspicion with a healthy dose of curiosity.

"Gideon Thorn?" the errand runner asked him.

"Mr. Thorn is not at home," Obi replied.

A standard Western Union envelope fluttered between the fingers of the young man's right hand as he said, "I'm s'pose to put this in his hand direct, like."

Glancing past him at the curbed bicycle, Obi answered, "Then you have a long journey ahead of you."

"Say what, now?"

"Mr. Thorn is traveling around the West. I cannot say exactly where he is today."

The runner thought that over, then said, "Well, then, why don't you go fetch the man of the house?"

Obi was torn between an urge to slap this upstart or to

laugh at him. Instead, straightfaced, he said, "I am a man. I occupy this house, and no one else is here."

That made the redhead frown, his mouth pinched to a narrow line. "Well, when does Mr. Thorn get back?"

Obi allowed himself a shrug. "Who knows? I have not seen him in a year or more."

"There's somethin' funny about this."

"Indeed. You have a message to deliver and be on your way, yet here you stand, still asking questions."

"Lookee here, now, boy—"

"We have established that I am a man, and not a boy. This is my home. If you prefer to leave without delivering the telegram, explain to your employer when you see him."

Now the young man's cheeks had turned an even darker pink. "You gonna make me say it, then?"

"Say what?" Obi Magoro challenged, though he knew perfectly well.

Through clenched teeth, out it came. "I oughta give it to a white man."

"Ah." Now Obi smiled, his least encouraging expression in his present mood. "If that is your employer's rule, then let me see it, written down."

"I don't take orders from no—"

"But if that is *your* idea, then, once again, I would invite you to explain it at the Western Union office. Perhaps they'll have you bring it back, if you are still employed by them."

The redhead clearly wanted to say more, to argue back, but all he said was, "Fine. You gotta sign for it."

"Indeed," Obi replied, fighting a childish urge to gloat.

The messenger produced a pencil stub and small notepad, scribbling the date and address before handing both across. He seemed surprised again when Obi signed his name in flowing cursive script and handed back the writing implements. At last, the flimsy Western Union envelope changed hands.

The errand boy was halfway to his bicycle when Obi called out after him, "Be careful on these streets, my son. There is no telling whom you'll meet."

The youth turned back to glare at him, half-muttering "I ain't your son," then mounted up and pedaled on his way, hunched shoulders rolling in time with his high-pumping knees.

A small thing, Obi thought, *but victory enough for now,* before he closed and double locked the heavy door.

The telegram, as he'd expected, was addressed to Mr. Gideon Thorn at the Pinckney Street address. Magoro did not recognize the sender's name—Josiah Lonergan—apparently residing in or near a town called Dillon, in the Colorado Territory.

Colorado.

He had been there once, running an errand for his mistress at that time, a task that had become his whole life's work. The very name—Spanish for "colored red," as he had come to understand it, in a reference to local stone and soil—filled him with apprehension of an evil bygone time. That feeling clung to him, increasing, as Obi began to read the message in his hand.

"Mr. Thorn," it started. "You don't know me but it's happening again. Stop."

Lowering the telegram, Magoro wished he could obey that last instruction, reading on no further. Memory was all he needed to recall the story's grim beginning, even though he had not witnessed the events first-hand. A small and passing tremor from his large hands made the paper rattle softly in his grip.

Nearly a quarter century had passed—in fact, it had been twenty-four years, now, marked by the recent birthday of his one true friend on Earth—since the events that shaped Obi Magoro's life. At that time, he had served Drusilla Thorn, descendant of the family patriarch who had transported him from French West Africa to Massachusetts after one of his big game safaris. At the time, Obi was already a man full grown, though he could not precisely peg his date of birth as white men reckoned it. He calculated that he must be close to forty-six years old by now, but time had never preyed upon his mind as it was wont to do with those of European stock.

Drusilla Thorn was on her own, a spinster, fabulously wealthy, when word came out of the West about the nephew she had never seen. Her brother, Aaron, had been toiling in the eastern foothills of the Rocky Mountains, building a new life away from Boston for himself, wife Felicity, and their two sons, Thomas and Gideon. One winter's night in 1854, in circumstances yet to be explained, the parents and their elder son were slaughtered by a home-invading creature that authorities suspected was a grizzly bear, although all local members that species should have been in hibernation or migrating into warmer regions at the time. Only the two-year-old survived that massacre, irrevocably marked a claw's track across his scalp, where his black hair was parted by a streak of white forever more.

By the time Drusilla Thorn learned of her loss, her nephew Gideon had landed at an orphanage in Lawrence—Colorado being, at that time, a part of Kansas Territory. Loath to travel farther than the finer restaurants of Boston, she'd dispatched Obi Magoro to retrieve her nephew, which became an odd adventure in itself, when he appeared among white Kansans bearing power of attorney from his mistress in the East. After a spate of telegrams, and intervention by the governor of Kansas Territory who had known Drusilla personally, Obi had departed with the child and learned his story on the train ride back to Boston.

On top of losing both his parents and his sibling, Gideon had suffered bullying by older children at the orphanage, humiliation that he was determined to expunge forever from his life. Obi had helped him there, with Aunt Drusilla's blessing, teaching Gideon the arts of Nguni stick-fighting, Dambe bare-knuckle boxing, and Engolo ritual combat. Meanwhile, Aunt Drusilla had enrolled her nephew at Weatherford Academy, then at Harvard University, where Gideon had graduated with a bachelor's degree in liberal arts, in 1873. Aunt Drusilla had died that same year, bequeathing her entire estate to Gideon, with the provision that he retain Obi Magoro.

By then, young Gideon would not have had it any other way.

Although accepted into Harvard's School of Law, Gideon had demurred, leaving Obi to manage his family home and fortune, with sage advice from the Boston Brahmin law firm of Messrs. Block, Enright & Sloan. His destiny, the sole surviving Thorn decided, was to seek the truth about whatever killed his parents and his brother—to find out, and if it lived, eradicate that monster from the planet.

He had failed at that, so far, but had continued rambling through the Wild West on his own, investigating other mysteries, reporting back to Obi at the house on Beacon Hill whenever he found time to write.

And now, this telegram from Colorado Territory, opening, "*It's happening again.*"

Magoro didn't need to ask what "it" was. Truth be told, he dreaded confirmation of his fear, but how could he report the message on to Gideon if he did not proceed, reading the telegram? To him, it did not constitute invasion of Thorn's privacy. Conversely, it could mean total disruption of the young man's life.

Or even end that life, itself.

Pouring a double brandy for himself, Obi Magoro took it to the mansion's study, sat down in his favored chair, and started reading from the top once more.

Mr. Thorn—You don't know me but it's happening again. Stop. I think you'll know exactly what I mean. Stop. I live outside of Dillon here and have or had a working ranch. Stop. All my hands have run off now due to this thing that comes around and kills them in the night. Stop. The sheriff reckons it's a grizzly like some others did in your day but my men all swear bullets won't stop this thing nor even slow it down to speak of. Stop. I'm ruined if we can't get rid of it somehow and others like myself besides. Stop. We've heard your story from a long time back and how you've tackled other things the law and such don't have a handle on. Stop. If you find it in your heart to help us you might find some peace and we can also put up a reward. Stop. I look forward to your speedy answer. Stop. Josiah Lonergan. Full Stop.

Obi Magoro's first impulse was to destroy the telegram. It was a moment's work to crumple it in one of his large hands, then strike a match and leave its ashes curling in the fireplace. He resisted that initial urge because he'd recognized his duty from the moment he began to read.

But how could he fulfill that duty?

True or false, he knew that Mr. Gideon would absolutely want to hear the news from Colorado Territory. In a sense, he had been waiting for it all his life, except for the two years before his family was ripped from him by night.

The problem, now, was that Obi Magoro only heard from Mr. Gideon sporadically, either by telegram or U.S. mail, the latter frequently delayed until Thorn had moved on from one location to another. Thankfully, railroad transportation of mail had begun the previous year, eliminating some of the delays inherent in travel by Pony Express, but some letters were still misrouted, and many smaller western towns still lacked railroad connections.

The best Obi could say of Mr. Gideon on any given day was that he must be somewhere in the West, address unknown until another missive found its way from Thorn to Beacon Hill—and by that time, he'd probably moved on, investigating yet another mystery or grisly crime.

Despite the latest telegram's apparent urgency, Obi Magoro simply could not reach out from his mansion on the hill to find Thorn anywhere he might be at a given moment. The last letter he had received from Mr. Gideon came postmarked out of Amarillo, Texas, summarizing an investigation there—suspected witchcraft that had come to naught—and saying that Thorn planned to "travel west" from there.

Which left an estimated 350,000 square miles of desert, mountains, and forest to cover before he reached California, and who knew where Thorn's curiosity and wanderlust might carry him from there?

The good news: Colorado Territory wasn't all that far

away, at least compared to Oregon or somewhere else he might decide to visit, based on word of mouth or clippings from an old newspaper. But proximity was relative, and while Obi Magoro waited for the next contact—hopefully by telegram, in which case he might have a swift chance to respond—all he could do was wait.

And in the meantime, work on *how* he would deliver the disturbing news, when it was time.

THREE

JUNE 5, 1876: SAN DIEGO COUNTY, CALIFORNIA

Riding out of the Mojave Desert, Thorn would have been happy if he didn't if he didn't see another cactus, rattlesnake, or sand dune for a good long while. The snakes had given him no trouble, really, glad enough to shy out of his way once he focused his full attention on them—and, in truth, he owed a debt of gratitude to certain cacti that stored water in their stems, providing vital moisture for himself, Shadow and Bell during the long ride west.

The desert wasn't dead and barren, as some writers commonly described it—quite the opposite, in fact—but Thorn agreed that it was merciless: baked by the sun all day, with temperatures commonly topping one hundred degrees, then plummeting to twenty overnight, and sometimes hitting zero at the higher elevations. As for life, both plant and animal, it was abundant, but the trend was toward venomous creatures and their prey, while flora armed itself with thorns, bristles, and spines.

So he was glad to see the last of it, if only for a little

while. His destination was a small town called Sagrado —"Sacred," when translated into English—but events over the past few weeks had not encouraged anyone who thought the settlement was blessed. Instead, from what he'd heard so far, they were inclined to think a curse had fallen over it and all inhabitants of the vicinity.

Thorn's first notice of the mystery had come to him while he was trailing Isham Winslow through Nevada, from a story in Reno's *Daily Nevada State Journal.* The article was brief, but mentioned farmers being found around Sagrado with their hearts torn out, no other seeming injuries except for superficial cuts and bruises. A second piece, published before he'd started south from Reno toward Las Vegas, offered names and dates, but added little more, beyond the fact that most of those inhabiting Sagrado and environs were both agitated and well armed, assuming bullets could protect them from the terror in their midst.

According to the *Journal,* victims of the predator—or predators—were taken after nightfall, sometimes within shouting distance of their homes. There had been four dead when Thorn started out of Washoe County, southbound toward his confrontation with the so-called man who raped and branded little girls, and more might well have fallen in the meantime, while he crossed the desert, trying to avoid a killing pace.

The dead, as far as Thorn knew, were Seymour Eastwood, Ranse McClure, Wesley Tannehill, and Heulet Carnes. None of the four had actually lived within Sagrado's posted limits, but their farms were close enough, their names and faces known to neighbors, for their sudden, grisly deaths to have the whole place up in arms. So far, neither Sagrado's marshal nor the county sheriff had accomplished anything worth wasting printer's ink in their attempts to apprehend the fiends responsible.

Or were the murders any human's work?

The *Journal* claimed each victim's heart had been "removed," but it stopped short of saying whether knives, bare hands, or fangs and claws had been employed to wreak the bloody havoc. Claims that none of those dispatched had suffered any injury from common scavengers when found, argued for human agency behind the deaths. But who would kill in such a fashion, targeting robust and able men who could—at least in theory—defend themselves?

That puzzled Thorn. In his experience, the kind of men who killed repeatedly for pleasure usually preyed upon women or children, as in Isham Winslow's case. It was a matter of convenience and strength, as well as any lust that might propel the killer in his choice of prey. Farmers were generally strong and wiry men, with ready access to firearms and other tools they could employ for self-defense at need.

And yet, in each case covered by the *Journal*—always granting that it could be wrong—the victims had been overpowered and subdued without much injury, before their hearts were taken, leaving each of them a castoff, lifeless husk. Furthermore, none of the hearts had been recovered from the murder scenes, suggesting that removal of that organ meant more to the slayer than a simple act of homicide.

What was the meaning of that mutilation? How and why was someone—or *something*—obsessed with taking human hearts?

By now, Thorn knew enough to stop him from assuming anything. Sagrado's killings might be murder—

meaning people killed by other people—or they might be something else entirely.

Which was why Thorn felt compelled to check it out.

He knew, as well as anyone—better than most—that there *were* monsters in the West. Some prowled in human form, like Isham Winslow. Others were entirely different, beyond the wildest alcohol-induced imagining of most frontiersmen, long accustomed as they were to violence in every form.

The beast that had attacked Thorn's family, for instance, or the dragon he had slain in Texas and the forest-dwelling creatures that had routed loggers from the wilds of northern California. Shakespeare had been correct, whether he'd known it at the time or not: *There are more things in heaven and earth, Horatio, than are dreamt of in your philosophy*.

Some seemed to come from dreams, while others brought nightmares to life.

Thorn caught his first glimpse of Sagrado shortly after noon, relieved that he could spend the night in town, a roof over his head, with food on hand that someone else had whipped up for a change. He would not start his prying into local secrets on arrival, rather waiting for a new day to begin his latest quest.

And if he found Sagrado running true to form with other towns he'd visited, he might not be entirely welcome there.

Marshal Orrin Pike was at his desk, sorting through WANTED posters from the day's mail, when he saw the stranger riding past his window, down the main street of

Sagrado. The town council had voted not to call the thoroughfare Main Street, but christened it Sagrado Boulevard instead, a name that Pike found both pretentious and ridiculous. It didn't qualify in his mind as a "boulevard," which sounded like a street you'd find in San Francisco, maybe in Chicago, and he thought if people didn't even know the town that they were riding through, to hell with them.

Pike stood and crossed the smallish office, hitching up his gunbelt as he went. His door was open, to relieve a measure of the heat that waited for him as he stepped outside. The stranger had already passed, but with the scarcity of traffic moving on Sagrado Boulevard these days, Pike had no difficulty tracking him, taking the new arrival's measure for himself.

The rider was a long, tall drink of water, all in black, though he could use a brushing-down to shake the trail dust. He looked young, somewhere in his mid-twenties, but he wore the pistols on his belt with all the confidence of someone who knew how to use them well. There was a Bowie on his belt, as well, around in back, and Marshal Pike scowled as he thought its blade would do nicely for cleaving through flesh and bone to reach a throbbing human heart.

Of course, Pike had no reason to suspect this new arrival in Sagrado was the one responsible for all his misery, these past few weeks. For one thing, riding in this way, the stranger stuck out like a second nose on someone's face. You couldn't miss him if you tried, all dressed up like an undertaker, packing iron.

Still, at the moment, when he had no leads at all toward solving any of the recent deaths among the people who depended on him, *everyone* was suspect. Hell, by now Pike reckoned half the folks in town suspected him as much as anyone.

And why not, when their normal lives of drudgery six days a week and Sundays off—if they were lucky—had been torn apart in such outlandish, gruesome style. If truth be told, Pike would've rather had a raid by hostile Indians or border trash. At least he understood that kind of violence. They all did, living in the hinterlands, so close to Mexico. But renegades and redskins had a motive, damn it. When they went to killing, it was all for profit or revenge against the white men who were squatting on their former hunting grounds. They hit and ran, without returning time and time again to mutilate a single victim, vanishing like ghosts without a trace.

Six murders, nearly identical, and all Pike had for evidence was one small boy—a Mexican, at that—who claimed the rancher that his parents worked for had been carried off and killed by giant birds. For Christ's sake, *giant birds*?

Sagrado had its share of eagles, absolutely, but who ever heard of one—much less a flock of them—that mobbed a full-grown man and killed him, then just took his heart and flew away? For that matter, who ever heard of eagles hunting after dark?

And if there had been such an eagle, could it have returned six times to one community, repeating its atrocious crime unseen, when every farmer in the neighborhood was riled up fit to bust?

The latest victim, Austin Lovett, had been slaughtered on his little spread southwest of town just four days earlier, picked off at night like all the rest. His missus had begun to wonder why he took so long feeding the stock, and when she'd gone to check on him, she found him out behind the barn, his shirt half ripped away, chest gaping like a bloody mouth and no heart nestled underneath his broken ribs.

So Marshal Pike would damn sure keep a sharp eye on the stranger who had stopped outside Sagrado's lone hotel, the Easy Rest, dismounting from his gray stallion and passing through the double doors in front. He must be staying, overnight at least, and that meant he'd be taking meals at McGuffy's restaurant, most likely stopping in at Joe Starbuck's saloon as well. Half of the folks in town would have their eyes on him by breakfast time tomorrow, and the marshal would be one of them.

And Pike would look for an excuse to have a private word while he was at it, learn the stranger's name and find out what brought him to town just now. It might be a free country, more or less, but to Pike's way of thinking, public safety trumped the right to privacy.

In fact, if all went well, he might just buttonhole the stranger when he went to McGuffy's or to Starbuck's, before he got settled down to sleep. There was no point in wasting time, Pike thought, when any night might drop another heartless body on his doorstep, making people in Sagrado wonder why in hell they even paid his salary.

The easy rest lived up to all Thorn's expectations for a hotel situated in a town Sagrado's size. The lobby wasn't richly decorated, but they kept it clean enough, with two well-padded chairs for guests to lounge in if they felt the need, watching the day unfold through windows facing on the street. A small bell overhead announced Thorn's entry, and a clerk of middle age emerged to man the registration desk, looking surprised to find he had a customer.

"Help you?" he asked, as if the thought were strange to him. Behind his wire-rimmed spectacles, faded blue eyes moved over Thorn, trying to figure out why he was standing there.

"I need a room," Thorn said.

"A room?" The clerk frowned, as he might have if someone had wandered in and asked him for a sack of groceries, or to come out and shoe a horse.

"A room," Thorn said again, confirming it. "This *is* a hotel, isn't it?"

After he blinked a time or two, the clerk replied, "Yes, sir! How long will you be staying with us?"

"I'm not sure yet," Thorn replied. "But if you're short of rooms—"

"No, no! Fact is, you have the whole place to yourself right now, except for me and Zelda. She's the housekeeper."

"In that case, I'll take something on the second floor, facing the street."

The clerk was nodding now, spinning a bulky register around and holding out a pen for Thorn to sign. "No problem, sir. The second floor it is, facing Sagrado Boulevard. Dollar a night seem fair?"

It was the first time any hotelier had asked for Thorn's opinion on the going rate. He nodded, said, "It's fine," and signed in neatly on the blank page facing him. "Business is slow, I guess?"

"Well, yessir, with... You know, with what's been going on."

"I read something about it," Thorn acknowledged. Then, deciding that it couldn't hurt to plant a seed, he said, "In fact, that's why I'm here."

The clerk immediately lost his smile. "How's that?" he asked, not bothering to add a "sir."

"Investigating," Thorn replied, keeping it vague. "It's what I do."

"You're with the sheriff's office, then? I mean, because they've been around before, and I don't see you wearing any kind of badge."

"Because I haven't got one. I'm not what you'd call a law enforcement officer."

"But, then—"

"I have another way of looking into things," Thorn said. "Sometimes it works. And if I waste my time, at least nobody's paying me."

"I'm not sure that I follow you."

"No problem." Thorn gave him a pair of silver dollars and inquired, "Where would I find the livery?"

"West end of town. Can't miss it, on your left."

And he was right. Thorn couldn't miss it, with the freshly painted sign out front announcing: LIVERY. The hostler was a man approximately twice Thorn's age, which put him somewhere in his early fifties, with a curly mop of graying hair. When Thorn went in, trailing his horse and mule, he caught another cautious look verging on rank suspicion, that reminded him immediately of the clerk back at the Easy Rest.

Unlike the man at the hotel, however, there was no confusion on the hostler's face as he quoted his rate of fifty cents per animal, per night. Thorn parted with another couple dollars and stayed on to help the man unload his mule, stashing the few provisions he had left after his trip across the desert. Once the hostler had unsaddled Shadow, walking him down to a stall with Bell next-door for company, Thorn wished them both good-night and started back to the hotel, bearing his saddlebags over one shoulder, with a rifle in each hand.

He got few looks along the way, simply because the town seemed nearly dead with sundown coming on. Most of the shops still wore their OPEN signs on doors or in their windows, but Thorn met no townspeople along the four-block trek back to the Easy Rest. If anyone was spying on him from the stores he passed, they kept well back and out of sight from passersby.

It didn't take a genius to tell Sagrado was a town scared stiff.

The hotel clerk gave Thorn another sharp look as he passed through with his trail gear, focused on the long guns he was carrying, besides the pistols on his belt. Thorn doubted that most guests who patronized the East Rest brought in that kind of firepower. In fact, he wondered when the last new guest had stopped at all.

Thorn climbed the stairs and found his room midway along the silent corridor. He leaned the Sharps rifle against a wall covered with paper in a flowered pattern, took his key out of a vest pocket, and let himself into the room. It wasn't large, but like the lobby, it was clean enough. The furniture included a brass bedstead, a chifforobe, a vanity complete with mirror and washbasin, with a chair set next to it. Thorn knew already that the hotel's privy was out back, a lamp and candles both provided for his comfort in the room, and just in case he made a hasty trek at night.

It didn't take him long, unpacking. Thorn had two spare shirts, some socks, a shaving kit, and that was all. Beyond those basics, he had ammunition in his saddlebags, together with the two newspaper clippings that had brought him to Sagrado in the first place, sniffing out a killer's trail.

Where it would lead him in the end, Thorn couldn't say. His "cases," as he called them, didn't always lead to a solution in the normal sense. If he could stop the killings, he'd be satisfied. But if he rode out having failed somehow, at least he'd know that he had done his best.

That wasn't much to offer people living in Sagrado, but they hadn't summoned Thorn, weren't even conscious of his stock in trade so far, and they'd have no right to begrudge him if he let them down.

But Thorn would hold a grudge against himself, in that event.

Failure came hard to him, beginning with the night he'd run away, leaving his parents and his brother to their brutal end. It mattered little to him that he'd been but two years old, and wounded at the time. He was a man now, with hard miles under his belt, and he would not be frightened off again.

But first, he needed sustenance.

Leaving his rifles in the chifforobe, Thorn locked the door behind him and went down to have a look at McGuffy's restaurant.

FOUR

Crossing the dry street toward McGuffy's restaurant, Thorn felt suspicious eyes upon him, but he didn't stop or look around, trying to pin them down. Sagrado Boulevard was clear as far as he could see, except for one man on a horse down by the livery, his back turned, leaving town as dusk closed in. Mounting the wooden sidewalk on the thoroughfare's far side, Thorn stepped up to the restaurant's doorway, passed through into a low-pitched hum of conversation—and immediately heard it stop.

Nine of the twenty-odd tables were occupied by couples or by men dining alone, all facing toward the doorway now, where Thorn stood backlit by the day's last red-orange light. Whatever some of them had been discussing, it was lost to mind now. Every person in the place, save one, was staring at him, not quite open-mouthed, but clearly with surprise.

The odd one out was young, a blond, wearing a gingham dress under an apron that presumably served as a waitress uniform. When Thorn entered, she'd finished lighting lanterns spaced around McGuffy's walls, but even she was thrown off-stride enough to let the match burn down until it stung her fingers, whereupon she gasped and dropped it to the floor, recovering to grind it out beneath one dainty shoe.

But her reaction time was short; Thorn gave her that. Before the customers had even thought of turning back to their unfinished meals, she crossed the room to greet him, putting on a smile that seemed nearly heartfelt. "Good evening, sir!" she chirped. "Party of one this evening?"

"As you see, Ma'am. By my lonesome."

Something in his tone or glance produced the next thing to a blush. She led him to a window table set for two, which let Thorn watch the street while physically discouraging most of the others from continuing to stare at him. Regardless, Thorn had no doubt what the topic of their conversations had been, cut short as suddenly as by the tremor of an earthquake underfoot.

"Our menu's on the wall," the waitress said. "If you have any questions..."

"What's good?" Thorn asked, deciding he would put her on the spot.

"It's *all* good, but the cook has made his special stew tonight. That's beef *and* pork, with every vegetable he could get his hands on. Comes with bread, and I can promise you, you won't leave hungry."

"Stew it is, then."

"And to drink, sir?"

"Coffee if you've got it. Black."

"I've got a fresh pot on right now." She smiled again, while barely glancing at his holstered guns, and added, "Be back with it in a jiffy."

"You know where to find me," Thorn said, smiling on his own account.

He left the other diners to their furtive looks and gossip, knowing what was on their minds. *Who's this guy? What's he doing in our town? Is he connected to the killings somehow? Does he even know what's going on?*

Well, they could wait and see, along with Thorn himself. Starting a case, he never knew where it would go, how he would handle it—or who'd still be alive when it was done, assuming that it was.

The coffee came, as black and strong as he had hoped. The stew, already made and piping hot, followed a couple minutes later, in one of the largest serving bowls he'd seen outside of wedding receptions in Boston. He dug in and was instantly rewarded by the mix of flavors, thinking he would have to leave the blond waitress a special tip.

Now, all Thorn needed was a short half hour to eat in peace, then maybe he'd stop into the saloon—Starbuck's, he'd seen—to have a nightcap, make some more heads turn, more conversations shudder to a halt.

A short half hour...

But Thorn guessed he wouldn't get it, when the door swung open and he saw a lawman standing there, staring at him.

"He's goin' in, just like you said, Marshal."

"Man's gotta eat," said Orin Pike, cutting a sidelong glance toward Charley Kuhn, his one and only deputy.

"We gonna go 'n check him out?" Kuhn asked, sounding a little too excited by the prospect of bracing a two-gun stranger dressed all in black. But he was young, of course. Pike hoped Kuhn would have time to learn from his mistakes.

Some didn't, and Pike reckoned that would be a crying shame.

"I might drop in," he said, in answer to Kuhn's question. "You've got rounds to make, doorknobs to rattle."

"But—"

"No buts, now. I know what I'm doin', Charley. Been at this a right long time."

And that was God's own truth. Sometimes it felt to Pike as if he's worn some badge or other and had been confronting strangers for a hundred years, instead of twenty-eight. In all that time, he'd killed two fellas who drew down on him, and one riding away after he'd robbed a small town bank. Pike hoped he wouldn't have to make it four. And most of all, he hoped the long, tall stranger wouldn't be the man who did for him.

It would be down to Charley then, to set things right, and Pike would bet a full month's pay he wasn't up to it.

"Now, Orrin—"

"Marshal."

"Right, sorry. I just thought, maybe, if we made a show of force..."

"No need to light a fuse," Pike said. "Specially when we still don't know what kinda man we're dealin' with."

"Well, if you're sure."

"Sure as I'll ever be. Get on about your rounds now, Deputy."

"Yes, sir."

Pike waited until Kuhn was on his way, clomping along the sidewalk toward the farther end of town, where he would stop and make his slow way back, checking on shops and offices en route. Most merchants in Sagrado lived upstairs, above their stores, but they still seemed to like a lawman coming by see that everything was buttoned up, and they'd forgotten nothing after closing time.

Pike stood awhile and thought about the stranger in McGuffy's, wondering about the best way to approach him. If he was a drifter, simply passing through, it wouldn't serve Pike's purpose to roll in, accusing him of anything or spilling too much information on the crimes that had Sagrado up in arms these past few weeks. Conversely, long experience had taught the marshal that he shouldn't be all smiles and sunshine, either. That could send a drifter the wrong message and encourage him to hang around, when otherwise he would've spent the night and then gone on his way.

So, forceful without making it a challenge some quick-trigger *hombre* felt a need to counter, turning up the heat. Pike would be reasonable and authoritative, without acting like the kind who throws his weight around just for the hell of it.

And he would keep the hammer thong unfastened on his Colt Peacemaker, just in case.

He crossed the thoroughfare slowly, almost reluctantly, and paused again before he let himself into McGuffy's, with its tantalizing smells. Stew night, Pike realized, and wished he could've had a piping bowl just then, instead of stepping off into the wild unknown.

Later for that.

He saw the stranger sitting by the window, eating stew himself, and spied the startling white streak in the young man's hair, along the center part. It wasn't dyed—who'd do a stupid thing like that, at twenty-something years of age? —which told Pike that it likely marked some kind of scar, although he couldn't figure out the cause.

Forget that, now. Stop staring at him and get on with it.

Pike saw Arlene, the waitress, headed toward him, but he waved her off and saw her pretty face adjust itself for trouble. For his part, Pike hoped she wouldn't see blood spilled this evening—especially not his.

Please, God.

He covered the short distance to the stranger's table, feeling others watching him, seeing the young man's eyes rising to meet him. Pike found nothing in the stranger's face to warn him whether he was jumpy, as most people were, when suddenly confronted with the law in new surroundings.

But he did look vaguely dangerous.

"You're new in town," Pike said by way of preamble, stating the obvious.

The stranger nodded, didn't speak.

Pike swallowed, tried again. "I thought we oughta have a talk. You mind if I sit down?"

Charley Kuhn looked calm enough, on the outside, but he was fuming as he walked away from Orrin Pike to make his first rounds of the night. Most days, Pike would be headed home at sundown, to the little house he shared with no one but his mongrel dog, maybe to have a drink and put his feet up after covering the town all day.

Of course, there hadn't been too many normal days over the past six weeks or so, not since the brutal killings started and they couldn't get a handle on the one or ones responsible. That rankled Kuhn, young as he was and inexperienced with much beyond the odd drunk raising hell on weekends, most of them cow hands or drifters passing through to patronize Starbuck's saloon. He knew some of the locals liked to pull a cork, as well, but they were smart enough to stay shut up behind closed doors, being damn sure they didn't get their Christian neighbors agitated, whispering behind their backs at Sunday services.

As if they needed any more to talk about, six people dead so far, and mutilated like some crazy man or heathen tribe might do for sport. New as he was to law enforcement, Kuhn still felt the way some townsfolk eyeballed him, the silent accusation in their eyes saying he should've done something by now to stop the terror, bring some human monster from the shadows, ready for a hanging rope.

And now, this stranger turning up had only made things worse.

Kuhn wished he were with Orrin Pike right now, staring the drifter down, demanding answers for his presence in Sagrado and how long he planned to stick around. The last thing people needed was another reason to be frightened in their homes, at work, and simply walking down the thoroughfare.

Okay, Kuhn knew that he was fairly green, didn't deny it, but he liked wearing a badge and gun, had loved the feeling of respect they'd brought to him before the murders started and the townsfolk changed from normal, reasonably happy-looking people into bleak souls who were wary all the time and kept their children close.

Since it began, Kuhn had been practicing in secret with his six-gun, making sure it was unloaded first, before he started fast-drawing against the mirror in his rented room at Mrs. Connor's boarding house. His speed was up to par, Kuhn thought, although he clearly wasn't ready to be facing someone like John Wesley Hardin, out of Texas. For Sagrado, on the other hand, Kuhn reckoned he was fast—although he actually hadn't drawn and fired against a human being yet, just rocks and cactus when he rode a safe mile out from town.

But close up, in a restaurant, with Marshal Pike beside him... Sure, he figured he could get the job done well enough.

Kuhn reached the far end of Sagrado Boulevard, peered through the window of Arbuckle's dry goods store, and saw nothing amiss. Turning back toward McGuffy's, he saw no one on the street and guessed that meant that Marshal Pike was already inside.

Kuhn left him to it, wished him well, determined that he'd keep his ears pricked for whatever sounds might indicate a ruckus going on. Gunfire would send him sprinting down the street toward who knew what, ready to stand or fall with Pike to save the town.

But Christ, he surely hoped it wouldn't come to that. Not now.

Most days, Kuhn barely felt he'd started living yet.

Thorn looked the lawman up and down, swallowed the stew he'd been chewing, and told him, "Suit yourself, Marshal."

The marshal sat across from him and said, "Sharp eyes you got. Some people don't bother to read the badge, first time we meet, and call me 'Sheriff' by mistake."

Thorn let that pass and asked, "You want something to eat?"

The marshal blinked at him. Replied, "Thank you, but no. Names Orrin Pike."

"Gideon Thorn."

"Can't say I've heard a you."

"No reason why you would have, Marshal. Not on WANTED posters, anyway."

"That's good to start with. Clears the air a bit."

"But not enough."

"Not quite. What brings you to Sagrado, Mr. Thorn?"

Thorn could have ducked the question, but he saw no reason to. Whatever fiction he might spin would be exposed the moment that he started asking questions around town. And so, he answered back, "The murders."

Orrin Pike had started working on a cautious smile, but now he lost it in a heartbeat. "You need to explain that."

Thorn spooned up another bite of the delicious stew and thought about the phrasing of his answer while he got it down. This wasn't his first confrontation with a lawman on the prod, worried about a town where things had suddenly gone terribly, inexplicably wrong. In Thorn's experience, their meeting could go one of two ways: Pike would bluster, threaten to expel him from Sagrado without any rightful cause, or they would come to terms, however grudgingly.

In either case, Thorn didn't plan to leave just yet.

"It's what I do, Marshal," he said by way of opening. "I travel, keep my eyes and ears open for what you'd call peculiar mysteries. When I discover one, I take a look around, investigate the circumstances, try to see what's going on. Sometimes it helps."

"And other times?"

"I ride out disappointed, wondering where I went wrong."

Pike, frowning, asked, "What qualifies you for that kind of work? What's your authority?"

"You asked two questions there. The first answer would be my personal experience. The second would be none, beyond what any citizen might have in dealing with an unsolved riddle."

"So, you're not a lawman."

"Never have been," Thorn replied.

"What makes you think that you can ride in here and solve what's kept me up nights for the past six weeks? What makes you better than the county sheriff and his deputies?"

"Nobody mentioned 'better,' Marshal. But I bring fresh eyes, where you've been staring down a long, dark tunnel, feeling lost. I may see something that you've missed. And if I don't, you've lost nothing."

"People in town and on the farms around Sagrado are afraid," Pike said. "Last thing they need right now's a stranger pokin' into things that don't concern him, when they've already lost friends and neighbors."

"Don't you think they'd have an interest in *why*?" Thorn countered.

"That's for lawmen to discover and decide. Suppose you somehow stumble onto those responsible for what's been happening. What, then?"

"You'll be the first to know," Thorn said.

"I got a deputy already," Pike replied. "Don't want or need another one."

"Sorry. Did you think I've come here applying for a job?"

That seemed to fluster Pike and gave Thorn time to eat more stew. After a moment, Pike said, "Look, I can't have strangers, amateurs, runnin' around town, gettin' in my way."

"No danger there, Marshal. I'd guess you've questioned everyone in town."

"Damn right."

"And if they think of anything before or after I have words with them, they'll come to you first thing...won't they?"

"Well..."

"I'm curious. That's all. And as I said, I've had some luck with other cases in the past."

"Such as?"

"Wire the Bates County sheriff's office in Missouri. Ask them if I helped out with the Lindsay family, last September."

Pike mulled that over for a second, then said, "Hey, you mean those cannibals?"

Thorn shrugged and let that go. "Or you could try Reginald Conklin. He's vice president of Siskiyou Logging. Try their office up in Sacramento, California."

"What'd you do for him?"

"I'll let him tell you that, himself."

"I'll think about contactin' them," Pike said. "Meanwhile, I've got no legal cause to run ya outa town."

"That's right. You don't."

"But I'll damn sure come up with somethin' if I start to think you're agitatin' folks for no good reason, makin' a bad business worse."

"That's never my intent."

"And I'll be watchin' you. Believe it, Mr. Thorn."

"Sounds good for both of us."

"We understand each other?"

Thorn considered that, then said, "You wear the badge. I hope for luck and don't do anything you wouldn't like. Is that about the size of it?"

"That's the *exact* size of it," Pike replied. "Don't make me sorry that I let you hang around."

With that, he rose and left. Thorn smiled, letting the diners who were gawping at him see it, then he turned back to the pleasant task of finishing his stew.

FIVE

Thorn finished off his stew in peace and left the waitress extra for the marshal's interruption of her evening. Outside, he found the town's half-dozen street lamps lit and challenging the night ahead. Sagrado Boulevard was totally deserted now, but windows set above its shops produced a homey glow the empty street belied. Another lamp was burning in the marshal's office, to his left, but Thorn had seen enough of lawmen for one night. He turned the other way and focused on Starbuck's saloon.

Piano music greeted him when he was still a block away, illumination spilling from the barroom's windows on both floors, and from around its bat-wing doors. The second-story rooms, he guessed—based on experience—would be for soiled doves to transact their business with men who wanted something more than cards and alcohol.

Thorn stood outside a moment, eyeballing the customers. Two poker tables were in use, by four men each, while half a dozen others ranged along the bar, sipping their beers or whisky shots. At one table, off to his left, two cowboy types were dickering with one of Starbuck's girls, perhaps discussing prices or the services available. Thorn took a chance and pushed his way inside, proceeding toward the bar without acknowledging the card players he passed. One of them watched him long enough to make another player nudge him, asking, "Is you gonna check or raise?"

The bartender was roughly Thorn's age, garters on his sleeves, a pale mustache hiding his upper lip. He paused in front of Thorn to take his order without too much glaring, then moved off to fetch his whisky and a mug of beer.

Beside Thorn, to his right, an older man who brought to mind a prospector was lecturing a younger one, who might have been a clerk at one of the assorted shops along Sagrado Boulevard. "I'm tellin' ya," he said, "the whole damn thing ain't natural. Ya know? Even the goddamn Chiricahua outa Arizona, over there, don't cut hearts outa people when they kill 'em. Scalps, awright, we all seen that, and maybe some a them there sexy bits, but *hearts*?"

The bartender returned and took Thorn's money with a nod, then told the lecturer, "You need to pipe down, Ned. You get folks all worked up for nothing, and we got a stranger here."

"Fer nothin'?" Ned shot back. "Did I jest hear ya say fer *nothin*'? Six men dead and more to come, sure as you're born, and you stand there—"

"I'll have to cut you off, unless you keep it down," the barkeep cautioned. Ned's companion seized that opportunity to slap him on the shoulder and depart.

Thorn edged a little closer to the older man. "Six dead, you say?" he asked.

Ned turned to scan him with one wary eye, the other washed out by a cataract. "You're new around here, ain't ya?" he inquired.

"I am," Thorn said. "But interested all the same."

"Uh-huh." The good eye narrowed just a bit, as Ned told him, "It's hard to keep on talkin' with my throat parched like it is."

"Let's fix that, shall we?" Thorn flagged down the barkeep, took a half-bottle of redeye off his hands, and steered Ned toward an empty table on the far side of the room, where they'd be relatively safe from eavesdroppers. The jangling piano laid down cover noise in aid of his design.

When they were seated, he told Ned, "I've kept up with the case from newspapers, the best I could while traveling. The last piece that I saw referred to four victims, but now you mention six?"

Ned downed a shot and poured himself another one before he spoke. "Yessir. Last one to go—so far, at least—was Austin Lovett. Workers found 'im out behind his barn, the heart torn outa him jest like the rest."

"How long ago was that?" Thorn asked.

Ned slurped his second shot and frowned. "What day's this, anyhow?"

"June fifth."

Ned started counting on his hands but quickly gave it up. "Call it about three weeks ago. And if ya wanna know the funny part—not *ha-ha* funny, but the strangest bit—a little Mex boy livin' on the Drummond spread—that's Randall Drummond, kilt before Lovett—claims he seen it all. Says it was giant birds that did the killin', if ya can believe it."

Giant birds. Thorn's mind turned to the Texas dragon for a second, but it hadn't dined on any special part of those it mangled, and with no hands to its name, much less a surgeon's skill, it couldn't have removed a heart without demolishing the torso that surrounded it.

"I take it that you're skeptical," Thorn said.

"Say what, now?"

"That you aren't buying the bird story."

"Well, now. I've lived around these parts for nigh on twenty years. Still lookin' for the lucky strike to set me up, but it's out there. I know damn well it is."

"Of course."

"But giant birds? Come one. I seen my share of buzzards, eagles, take your pick. I even seen a condor once, I swear to God. O' course, a condor's just a bigger kinda buzzard, if ya didn't know. They mostly feed on carrion, and sure as hell to go 'round killin' men to get their hearts."

"So far," Thorn said, "I understand the victims have been farmers in the area. Nobody's been taken from town."

"Not *yet,*" Ned answered, as he poured himself another shot. "But who or whatever it is, they's gonna come up short of farmers purty soon. Another six or seven spreads within a few miles of Sagrado, and it's all dried up. Ya see? They's gonna have to come in town, to keep on killin' like they is."

"And you feel safe, out on your claim?"

Ned's face turned to a mask of frank suspicion then. "Why would ya ask a thing like that? You got no damn idea where my claim is, do ya?"

Thorn smiled. Replied, "I only meant, working alone out in the countryside, you must have thought about..."

"Gettin' my own heart took? Hell, yeah, I *thought* about it. But I keep a ten-gauge close to hand, loaded with buckshot. Anybody tries to mess with me, his mama wouldn't know 'im when I's done with 'im."

"About those murder scenes," Thorn said, holding his

smile as his companion drank another shot. "Could you, by any chance, direct me to the places where the crimes occurred?"

Charley John was lurking in an alley separating Havelock's Hardware from Tom Foley's legal office, watching Starbuck's from the shadows there. He liked to hide at times, when he was on the night shift, just in case one of Sagrado's citizens got up to something fishy, thinking nobody could see him in the dark. Between walking patrols, it was Kuhn's practice and his pleasure to become obscure, invisible, and see the small town from a new perspective. What was going on behind closed doors, drawn blinds, where prying eyes were not supposed to penetrate?

Tonight, he had his eye out for the stranger dressed in black.

He'd tracked the tall man from a distance as he left McGuffy's, scanned the empty street outside, then ambled down to Starbuck's for a drink. Kuhn didn't know the stranger's name yet, hadn't talked to Marshal Pike since they had separated earlier, but he assumed that Orrin would've jailed the stranger right off, if he'd shown up on a WANTED poster at the office. Anyway, before the night was over, Kuhn supposed he drop into the Easy Rest Hotel and have a word with Arvid Chesney, on the night shift over there.

But name or no name, he was on the stranger's trail now, waiting for the man in black to take one step across the deadline in Kuhn's mind, then he would swoop down and arrest him, haul him in for good old-fashioned questioning.

Of course, he'd need a decent reason first, so Orrin didn't get fired up and snatch his badge away. He'd gotten used to it, the slight weight on his shirt, the Colt snug on his hip, and the authority that came along with them to let Kuhn count himself as special, someone set apart from other men.

He checked his pocket watch, emerging from the alley just a step or two, to read its face by lamplight, and discovered that the stranger had been inside Starbuck's for the better part of half an hour now. Did he have an epic thirst to quench, or was he randy from the trail, headed upstairs with whoever was putting out tonight? Maybe redheaded Julianne, or brunette Monica. What was the blonde's name? Della? No, Delvinia, with the exotic twist.

And there was one more possibility. He might have fallen into conversation with a local who had thoughts to share and tales to tell.

Who might that be? Charley considered walking past Starbuck's and peering through the window, but that felt too obvious—and what would happen if the stranger left just as he happened by? Should Kuhn confront him then, keeping it casual, in spite of Orrin's order to back off? And if he saw the man in black but kept on walking, without speaking, would it mark Kuhn down as strange? Maybe convince the stranger he was under scrutiny?

The deputy decided he would give it ten more minutes, but in fact, he didn't have to wait that long. Before half the allotted time had passed, he saw the stranger leave Starbuck's and spend another moment on the sidewalk, taking in the night air, killing time, before he struck off toward the Easy Rest.

Kuhn didn't follow right away, particularly when he saw the stranger walk around in back of the hotel, likely to use the privy there. The trick to spying, after all, was not to be observed while you were doing it. The stranger hadn't seen him yet, and might not even know there was a deputy in town. That made surprising him a little easier, if it was necessary down the line.

Kuhn thought about his weapons next: twin Colts, together with the Bowie on his belt, and what about the two rifles he'd brought back from the livery? The Winchester was common in Sagrado, even more so on outlying farms, but there had also been a longer weapon, possibly a Sharps, inside a supple buckskin case with just a portion of its stock exposed.

Some kind of hunter, possibly. But what would be his prey?

No matter how he tried to think his way around it, Kuhn kept coming back to bodies with their hearts carved out.

He would ask Orrin more about it in the morning, see if he could subtly find out what the marshal had found out about their new arrival, talking to him in the restaurant. No doubt, he'd get another warning not to rile the stranger, but that didn't mean Kuhn couldn't do his basic duty as a lawman. He was paid to watch out for the people of Sagrado, keep the peace among them, and prevent all manner of disturbances.

Granted, that hadn't worked out lately, with the corpses piling up, but Kuhn thought every mystery had a solution, if you dug down deep enough.

He checked his watch again, decided that the man in black should have cleaned up by now and slipped in through the Easy Rest's backdoor. Taking his time, Kuhn started down the street to have a chat with Arvid Chesney, get the stranger's name at least, and find out what else he could learn.

A new clerk was on duty when Thorn got back to the Easy Rest, but he had done his homework on the only guest in residence and greeted Gideon by name, trying a smile that didn't seem to fit his long and freckled face below its thatch of ginger hair. Thorn nodded as he passed and went upstairs, pausing outside his room to test the lock, then let himself inside.

The room was as he'd left it, tidy, with his rifles still secure inside the chifforobe. If anyone had come by snooping in his absence, they had managed not to make a mess while they were at it. Thorn had no good reason to suspect a prowler, but in his experience, with nervous residents and lawmen on the prod, most anything was possible.

He locked the door behind him, wedged it with the bedroom's only chair, and slipped out of his suit while he considered what he'd learned from old Ned—last name Templeton, as it turned out—before he left Starbuck's and started back to the hotel. He'd read the names of four victims before arriving in Sagrado, and the latest two, while formerly unknown to him, did not come as a great surprise. All farmers living in the open countryside so far, but their numbers were thinning out as Ned explained it, sparking worry that the killer might begin to strike in town if he—or *it*—ran short of victims on the plains.

And, then again, the man or thing responsible might simple choose a change of scene at any time, moved by a whim.

Six farms, and all had been picked over by the county sheriff's office, with whatever help they would accept from Marshal Pike. That said, Thorn thought his best chance of discovering new evidence—or learning anything of use at all—would come from visiting the last attack's location, on the Lovett farm.

As Ned explained it to him, Austin Lovett was—had been—a lifelong bachelor. He had two or three farmhands he'd paid to help around the spread but they had scattered when he died and took all hope of future payment with him. There was no one currently in residence, which meant Thorn ought to have a chance to look around without disturbing anybody or inviting further questions from the law.

If that failed, he proposed to take the other farms in a reverse order, moving on to Randall Drummond's spread. Drummond had been a childless widower, if Ned had it aright, and his ranch was still inhabited by a small Mexican family, keeping the livestock duly supervised. That family included one child Ned described as "little Enzo," who had witnessed part of Drummond's death and claimed that his attackers had been "giant birds."

All told, Thorn had a fair amount of ground to cover, and he also hoped to speak with leading figures in Sagrado, maybe starting with the doctor, possibly the preacher at the town's sole church. He didn't put much stock in ministers, per se, finding them just as venal as the members of their flock, if not more so. But preachers soaked up secrets as a sponge held water. If he could induce the reverend to talk, Thorn might learn much about Sagrado, its inhabitants, and maybe the calamity that had befallen them.

And failing all of that...then, what?

In other cases, Thorn had simply made himself available, serving as bait to draw some human murderer or otherworldly predator out of the shadows, into killing range. Word of his inquiries would circulate around Sagrado soon. Indeed, his presence there, already known to law enforcement and observed by various civilians, should be gossip fodder by the time he went to breakfast in the morning. Someone might approach him with opinions on the crimes, or else, if privately involved, start scheming to eliminate him as a threat.

In either case, he thought, it would be more than he had now, just names on paper and the circumstances of their ghastly deaths.

As Thorn prepared for bed, he started checking off the things that likely could not be responsible. Not ghosts, for one. Sagrado had no reason to be haunted—or, at least it hadn't, when the murders first began. And not a cousin of the Texas dragon, which would not have been mistaken for a flock of giant birds—plural, he noted—even by the youngest child. Not creatures like the ones he'd met in northern California, as no forests stood nearby to shelter them, and they would instantly be spotted roaming over open ground.

As he lay down to sleep, his Colts and Bowie close at hand, Thorn's mind was leaning toward a human hand behind the slayings, but that still left much to be explained, beginning with the "giant birds" allusion from the only living witness to one of the crimes.

It was too much to process at the moment, and he closed his eyes, hearing distant piano music coming out of the saloon. Thorn lay, waiting for sleep, and hoped he would not dream.

SIX

Hayden Brokaw set his fork down by his supper plate and listened to the squealing from his hog pen. Its eleven occupants were usually quiet after sundown, when he's finished slopping them, but they had started in clamoring now, and he could hear at least one of them butting up against their pen's plank fence.

"I'd better see what's riled them up," he said, rising reluctantly from his unfinished pot roast, Letha's special Sunday dish. They had leftovers on this Monday night, but that was just as good, with fresh-made gravy on the meat.

"I'll help you, Pa," Daniel chimed in, already springing from his chair. At ten years old, he always sought to help around the farm, and Hayden knew that made him lucky, after hearing tales of kids who moaned and groaned over the slightest bit of work.

"No need, son," Hayden told him, seeing instant disappointment on the boy's tanned face. "I'll be right back."

"Sit down, young man, and finish eating," Letha added. And to Hayden, "You be careful, now."

"You know I will."

It was the murders on her mind, he knew, as they were haunting everyone around Sagrado since the killing started, going on and on. Before he left the four-room house, Brokaw put on his working hat and fetched his Model 1866 Winchester—dubbed the "Yellow Boy" for its receiver, made of alloyed brass and bronze—down from its wall pegs by the door.

He kept a live round in the rifle's chamber, with the hammer down, his wife cautioned to touch it only in the case of an emergency, and Daniel warned under a promise of a hiding that he mustn't *ever* touch the weapon unless Hayden placed it in his hands and ordered him to shoot at something. No mistakes allowed when life and death were riding on the line.

Speaking of which, before he left the warmth and light of home, Brokaw told Letha, "Better put the latch on, Sunshine. I'll knock when I'm finished, so you'll know it's me."

That worried look was still on Letha's face, but she hopped to it, answering, "Just as you say, Hayden."

Once he was outside, the farmer stood and waited till he heard the solid latch engaged, then dropped the smile he's worn indoors to keep his loved ones calm, took a two-handed grip upon his Winchester, then set off to discover what in hell had spooked his hogs.

It could have been most anything. Coyotes were the safest bet, and he never gave a thought to any kind of snake, because the hogs would eat them and they were immune to rattler venom anyhow. Of course, a cougar might be passing through, looking to snag itself an easy meal, and nine or ten months earlier, Hayden had seen a grizzly bear while he was plowing up his southern field for corn. The great beast barely glanced at him from fifty yards away, and never broke its rolling stride as it continued on its way toward Mexico.

But now, preoccupied with the god-awful murders, Brokaw worried that it might be something else riling his pigs. He'd personally known the third man killed, poor Wesley Tannehill, who'd left a wife and three young ones, forced off the land of course, because they couldn't keep it up or pay for help.

Not me, he told himself, as he approached the hog pen, noting that the pigs inside were quiet now, but still shifting uneasily. *Not me, by God.*

If he found anyone or any*thing* trespassing on his homestead, Brokaw meant to shoot and keep on shooting, never mind the questions afterward. Folks in the neighborhood knew damned well, after all the trouble, that they should stay home at night, or carry lights at least, and call out ample warnings, if they had to travel after dark. Anybody who came creeping in around the farms at night—or even in Sagrado, he suspected, after six men killed—was simply begging to be laid out cold and dead.

A sudden thought occurred to Brokaw then. The county had a nice reward, five hundred dollars, offered up to anyone who helped the sheriff's office solve the murders. Brokaw thought that kind of money would go far toward seeing him and Letha through the winter, coupled with the income that he hoped to make from selling off his produce in the fall.

Some might have called it blood money. To Hayden Brokaw, it was all the same, whether her cashed in on coyote pelts or brought a killer down. It could be payday and a public service, all rolled into one.

With that in mind, there was a certain jauntiness to Hayden's steps as he approached the sty.

“I shoulda gone with Pa," Daniel complained, pushing the food around his plate, not eating now.

"You heard him," Letha said. "He wanted you inside." Then, as a sop to wounded feelings, she tossed in, "Protecting me."

She noticed Daniel's chest puff out a little and took care to mask her smile. It lasted for a second, then her son began to say, "But what if—"

"What if nothing," she spoke up, cutting him off. "Your father's smart and strong, he's armed, and it's no more than forty paces to those smelly pigs."

"They're mighty tasty, though," Daniel replied, and in that moment sounded so much like his father that it nearly brought a tear to Letha's eye.

"We're selling most of them, you know," she said.

"Oh, sure. But keeping two to breed and one to eat, Pa says."

Cautiously, with eyes downcast, she asked him, "Danny, does it ever bother you, raising the piglets up to go that way?"

"No, Ma'am," he quickly said. "It isn't like as they were dogs. Say, if we had a dog—"

"We'll talk about it with your father," she said, thinking that a good watchdog, or even two, would be a help these nights, when there was death afoot and murder on the wind. Not pure-bred fighting dogs, but good-sized mutts with sense enough to raise a racket if intruders came sniffing around. A dog or two that she could sic on strangers should the need arise.

"Pa's been a while now, don't you think?" asked Danny.

"Not so long. The hogs are quiet now, you hear?"

"So, why isn't he back?"

"Having a look around, I should imagine. Making sure that everything's all right before he comes back to his supper—as you should be eating yours."

Too old to pout these days, Danny just frowned and ate a piece of tater to appease her, chewing as if it required his total concentration, even though she knew his mind was outside, with his father in the dark.

And hers was, too. Not just her mind, but Letha's heart as well.

She had been frightened, naturally, when the first murder occurred. Most thought it had been drifters passing through, or possibly a Chiricahua war party, despite the lack of any sign that redskins were involved. The toll struck three before a man she personally knew and liked was snatched away, and now she barely slept at all for fear of men or unknown monsters lurking in the night.

"Maybe we ought to fetch the Colt," Danny suggested.

"Why? So we can shoot your father, coming in?"

"No, Ma'am! I meant..."

He let it trail away, but Letha knew *exactly* what he meant. Besides the Winchester, Hayden had an old Colt 1861 Navy Revolver in the bedroom, tucked inside his nightstand's drawer. He'd taught her how to shoot it, and right now she wished to have that gun in hand, but Letha reckoned it would frighten Danny more and signal that she didn't trust his father, her husband, to keep them safe.

"Just give him time," she urged her son. "He's only been outside a minute, and it's no good panicking."

"No, Ma'am."

"When he gets back and tells us nothing's wrong—"

A rifle shot rang out, blasting whatever Letha meant to say out of her mind.

"*Xib tal*," Gabor cautioned, watching the white man's shadow stretch before him with the lamplight from the house behind and moon glow forcing it to veer off to one side, as if his spirit were already leaving him, seeking a new home in the universe.

"Man coming."

And behind Gabor, he heard the rustling of feathers, so like autumn leaves when agitated by the wind. He shot a glance in that direction, stern-faced, and was not required to order silence. Instantly, feeling his eyes upon them, his companions froze in place as if they had been turned to stone. Eyes gleamed beneath their domed brows, over curved beaks, watching him and waiting for his next command.

The white man came prepared for trouble, or imagined that he did. The weapon in his hands was dangerous, but he had no idea of whom or what lay waiting for him in the shadows of the night. Nervous he must be, after all the harvesting before, yet he was coming to present himself for slaughter, all the same.

Kisin would welcome him as he'd been happy to accept the other interlopers' contributions, roused by their resistance and uplifted by their final agony. The elements were all in place, the stars nearly aligned.

And soon, with any luck, it would be finished. Then, Gabor could rest from his unceasing labors and ascend to his reward.

The knife he held was curved and razor-sharp, its blade scoured with sand after the last blood sacrifice. Wielding it properly was an acquired skill—no, an *art*—drilled into him from childhood when the prophecy declared him chosen for the greatest task in all of human history.

Not that the whites were truly human, in Gabor's eyes. They were treacherous, deceitful thieves who had wreaked havoc with his people, cost them everything on Earth that ever mattered to them. But the time was coming for a change. Gabor could feel the call to battle thrilling in his blood, sense the imposing weight of his responsibility that anchored him to *Mamah Lu'um,* his Mother Earth.

The trick, defeating armed white men, was to negate their weapons at the onset, trick them into letting down their guard, then strike with all the righteous fury of a *xtaabay*—a demon seeking blood and holy retribution for their countless crimes. That retribution would be ruinous, and at the same time, it would save the world they had despoiled.

Gabor admired the wisdom and tenacity of Nature, wherein all things found their proper balance, given time.

Hayden Brokaw wouldn't have admitted it to anyone—well, maybe Letha, if they'd been tucked up in bed and drifting off toward sleep—but he was damn well nervous, edging toward afeared now, as he crossed the farmyard toward his pigsty, drawing farther from the reassuring lights of home, with just a waxing crescent moon above. Though it was cool outside, his palms felt slippery from clinging to the Yellow Boy, and Brokaw took turns wiping one and then the other on his denim pants.

"Most likely nothing," he advised the night, half whispering, but Lord, it didn't feel like nothing, out there in the dark. He would have liked to double back and lock himself inside the farmhouse with his loved ones, but it wasn't what a real man did when danger came to call, regardless of the hour. It would frighten Letha more than she already was, and set a horrible example for his son.

Off-hand, there was no reason why the deadly prowler should have chosen his farm for the next attack—but, then again, there'd been no reason anyone could make out for the other farmers to be butchered as they were. He knew, or knew of, at least half a dozen other men with spreads around Sagrado, each as likely to be taken as himself, but when you looked at them by moonlight, those weren't odds he'd care to put his money on.

As a precaution, Brokaw cocked the hammer on his Winchester, saving a second, maybe two, if he was forced to use the rifle in a hurry. Its .44-caliber rimfire rounds packed a wallop, sending a heeled bullet hurtling down range at 1,125 feet per second, according to the sales brochure. In practice, that meant approximately half an ounce of solid lead striking the target with 568 foot-pounds of energy. Brokaw was hazy on the math behind it, but in practice, he could say that anything he'd ever aimed at with the Yellow Bow had promptly dropped down, dead.

So that was good, at least, assuming that he got a chance to use it in the first place. All the other victims so far had been men, Brokaw assumed, who were accustomed to defending hearth and home with any force required.

And that was something else: why was it only one man taken down per farm, leaving their families and any hired hands unmolested? Even with the kid who claimed he'd seen something the night that Randall Drummond died, he'd come away from it unharmed.

And babbling about "giant birds," whatever in hell *that* meant.

Tonight, Brokaw was worried about people coming on his land, threatening him, if not his family per se. Of course, if he was gone...

"Stop that right now," he warned himself, aloud. A couple of the hogs peered at him through their fence slats, but the rest were on the far side of the pen, snuffling at something over there.

And what was *that* he saw moving around, beyond the sty?

"Somebody there?" Brokaw demanded, in his most intimidating voice, although he had to grant there was a tremor to it that he didn't like at all. "Come outa there where I can see you, or I'm gonna blow you full of holes."

Another slightly shifting movement, but nobody stepped into the clear.

Taking his time, edging around the pen, Brokaw had the Yellow Boy shouldered and ready to fire at the first sign of trouble besides murky shadows.

"Last time I'm warning you!" he said, raising his voice a bit, but not enough to rattle anyone back at the house, in case his eyes were playing tricks on him. They might well be, in fact, and being scared was no excuse, in Brokaw's mind, for acting like a fool.

His boots scuffed on the soil as he began circling around the sty. It reeked, of course, that was hog's pen for you, but was there *another* scent beneath the obvious? He frowned, keeping a sharp eye on his rifle's sights, and speeded up his walking pace a bit.

Yes, he was definitely smelling something now, besides pig slop and what they turned it into after chowing down, but Brokaw couldn't put his finger on it. Sweat, maybe, besides his own? That wasn't coming from the hogs, or any other animal that he could think of, standing there.

But if—

A sudden, rustling movement to his right made Brokaw turn in that direction, rifle tracking off across the sty and toward his barn. Something was definitely on the move, man-sized, if not in any shape he could associate with human kind.

"I warned you twice, goddamn it," he rasped out, and squeezed the trigger, welcoming the gun's recoil against his shoulder. "How's that now? Feel good?"

Before he had a chance to pump the rifle's lever-action, though, another rush of movement came directly at him from the front—a really large shape, or perhaps group of prowlers, bearing down upon him at a sprint, the only sounds a louder rustling—*feathers? Jesus, can it be*—and footsteps on the hard-packed ground.

A solid weight slammed into him and bore him backward, downward, as he felt the rifle twisted from his grasp. The shot would have alerted Letha, sent her running for the pistol to defend herself and Danny, but if Brokaw was the only target, they'd be wise to stay inside, behind closed doors.

He fought and squirmed, trying to grapple free, but couldn't move his arms or legs worth anything. He was engulfed by something musty-smelling—yes, feathers, by God—and then, against the dark sky overhead, he saw a flash of what he took for steel. It rose, then fell at an appalling speed and ripped into his chest, shearing through flesh, muscle, and bone.

Before it finished him, Hayden Brokaw had time for one last scream. That done, the stars above began to flicker out, and then were gone.

SEVEN

JUNE 6, 1876: BOSTON

Obi Maroro never worried, in the normal sense. He'd seen and done too much during his life—in Africa, and then in the United States—to think that dwelling on a problem would resolve it automatically and make it go away. In fact, he knew the very opposite was often true. Try to *forget* a problem, and solutions might suggest themselves in time, like bubbles rising in a swamp where nothing had been visible before.

Unfortunately, he could not put Gideon out of his mind, much less the telegram that was inviting Thorn to make another pass through Colorado Territory, hunting for the thing that killed his family almost a quarter-century before. However much he longed to turn away from it, it was his duty to inform Thorn of the strange communication and allow the young man to proceed as he saw fit.

But how?

One possible approach, while not his favorite, was to contact the legal firm of Messrs. Block, Enright & Sloan, trustees of the Thorn fortune, Boston Brahmins of impeccable credentials, with lavish offices downtown near the city's recently completed Post Office Square. That was a three-stage process, starting with a message that requested an appointment that would never be refused, considering the late Drusilla Agnes Thorn's very substantial fortune.

Once he'd scheduled the appointment, Obi had to schedule transportation from the house on Beacon Hill to his intended destination. Only one cab service in the city would accept black passengers, and only then if they were well supplied with cash. His driver would be black, of course, and that meant taking care to agitate no whites along the way, particularly Irish of the lower working class who missed no opportunity to take offense at blacks, Chinese, Italians—anyone, in fact, whom they regarded as "inferior."

Finally, there came arrival at the firm, his cab waiting outside, while Obi verified his personal appointment with the partners to a frowning doorman, then was shown into a waiting room where no white client ever spent a moment of his time. Whichever of the partners met with him at last, they'd take a special passage to that worthy's office, making sure to meet no other clients while en route.

The whole procedure would have been much different if Gideon was going in to see the firm's leaders, but this was Boston in the midst of an election year, when candidates were falling all over themselves with plans to end Reconstruction in Dixie and strip former slaves of the few civil rights they'd achieved since Appomattox.

As he climbed the marble steps to reach his destination, with the doorman tracking him, Obi Magoro hoped he might obtain some lead to Mr. Gideon's last known address out west. With that in hand, he could attempt to reach

Thorn personally and impart the message that he carried folded in his pocket.

Failing that, he would return home to the house on Beacon Hill and bide his time.

SAGRADO, CALIFORNIA

Thorn was looking forward to his breakfast at McGuffy's, braced to let the other early diners ogle him until they tired of it, as long as no one physically intruded on his private space. The gun belt that he wore under his black frock coat would almost certainly deter that, and he hoped that Marshal Pike had seen enough of him last night to let him eat in peace.

There was more traffic on Sagrado Boulevard this morning, merchants opening their stores and sweeping off the sidewalks, half a dozen wagons bringing merchandise or bearing shoppers from outlying farms to stock up on supplies. When he had finished breakfast, Thorn would check on Bell and Shadow at the livery, then start his rounds with questions that some locals might refuse to answer, coming from a stranger. Still, Thorn knew he would learn nothing if he didn't ask.

A new waitress was serving customers when Thorn entered McGuffy's, this one a brunette who didn't seem to notice that the buzz of conversation in the room dropped off to whispers instantly. Smiling her way across the room, she greeted Thorn and led him to another window table looking out upon the thoroughfare, directing his attention to a breakfast menu on the large wall-mounted slate.

Thorn ordered two fried eggs, biscuits and gravy, with a

slice of ham and fried potatoes on the side. Coffee came first, and in the meantime, Thorn decided that this morning's diners seemed even more pensive than the ones he'd interrupted at their dinners, yesterday. He wondered why, and asked the waitress when she came back from the kitchen with his steaming coffee mug.

"Oh, sir, you haven't heard?" Her smile had faded, and she had a vaguely haunted look around her violet eyes. "There's been...another one."

"Another one?"

"Yes, sir." Her voice dropped to a stage whisper, as she glanced left and right, in search of lurking eavesdroppers. "Another *murder*. Like the others, sir."

Thorn didn't have to ask what that meant. Wearing an expression of commiseration, he leaned closer, barely whispering himself. "Who was it this time?"

"Well..." Another hasty look around, before she answered him. "They say it's Mr. Brokaw. Lived out with his wife and son, due west of town about two miles. I didn't know them well, you know, but they've been in a time or two since I've been working here, for lunch when they were shopping. Little Danny liked to order griddle cakes, regardless of the time."

"And once again, no injury to wife or child?" Thorn asked.

"None that I've heard of, sir."

Another diner clinked his spoon impatiently against an empty coffee mug, and she went bustling off to serve. Thorn stared out at Sagrado Boulevard until his meal arrived, then dug in with a will, enjoying every bit of it, surprised to find his ham slice was the size of a small steak. Eating allowed his mind to roam farther afield, planning his day and wondering how soon he could afford to call upon the widow Brokaw at her farm.

Too much intrusion on her grief would be offensive, possibly resulting in another visit from the marshal. Pike still had no legal cause to run Thorn out of town, but in an agitated atmosphere approaching panic, none might be required. Even if Thorn was left alone by lawmen, other locals might decide the stranger had outlived his welcome in their town, and fending off attacks from outraged townsmen would defeat his purpose at the start.

No, Thorn decided, he would start in town, where he could think of several persons who might have some insight on the recent crimes. Sagrado had a doctor, undertaker, and a minister. Thorn didn't know their names yet, but he meant to learn, and introduce himself to them without needless delay.

Sagrado's sole physician was a Doctor Reuben Baldridge, operating from an office next-door to a millinery shop that Thorn imagined must be struggling to stay alive. He counted seven hats displayed in its front window, men's and women's, all apparently handmade, of decent quality, but dusty from the time they'd spent untouched. When Thorn bent closer, checking out their prices, he knew why.

The doctor's office smelled of alcohol and something else, perhaps a latent whiff of ether from a room somewhere in back. A miniature cowbell clanked once as he entered, and a male voice called out from the rear, "I'll be right there."

When Doctor Baldridge showed himself, he proved to be a man of thirty-some-odd years, with curly hair he'd tried in vain to comb, wearing gray flannel slacks, a vest to match, and a white shirt. Thorn had already seen his suit coat hanging on a peg behind what might have been a receptionist's desk, if one had been employed.

"A new face," Baldridge said, approaching him, "and not a sickly-looking one, I'm glad to say." He shook Thorn's hand and introduced himself, adding, "I guess you'd be the stranger everybody's curious about."

"That obvious?"

"All strangers stand out in Sagrado, as you might suspect. Add timing, with the murders and the rest of it—" a glance at Thorn's twin Colts—"and I would classify you as...unique."

"Is that a compliment, or..."

"Yet to be determined. You are...?"

"Sorry. Thorn. My first name's Gideon."

"A hewer, from the biblical translation," Baldridge said. "Someone who cuts things down. A man of war, perhaps."

"I can't say that I've ever studied up on it," Thorn lied. "Right now, I'm an investigator, of the private kind. I'm hoping you can tell me something in relation to the recent crimes."

"To what end?"

"Stopping them, maybe. Or solving them, at least."

"Where Marshal Pike and Sheriff Coleman haven't managed to?"

"I bring fresh eyes and different experiences that might help."

"Such as?"

"I wonder whether you'd believe me, if I told you."

"Something supernatural, perhaps? Don't look surprised, sir. Fear breeds strange ideas, and they're all over town."

"Right now, I'm trying to pin down some details on the crimes."

"As in, how did the victims die?"

"To start with, yes. I read about the hearts, of course."

"In which case, there's not much that I can add," Baldridge replied. "I knew a couple of the farmers as my patients, though I only saw them here on rare occasions. Afterward...well, there was nothing I could do for them."

"You saw the wounds, though?"

"With the marshal and our undertaker, Elmo Dickson, yet."

"And your opinion, if you don't mind, on the way their hearts were taken?"

Baldridge thought about that for a long moment, then shrugged. "Well, I suppose there's no harm telling you. It's not a case of confidentiality, by any means. The hearts were rather skillfully removed, by carving that would be. I wouldn't point the finger at a surgeon, if we had one, naturally. Any butcher could have done it, or a hunter used to dressing out his kills."

"Not torn out by an animal."

"Certainly not. Unless you know of some strange animal that's learned to handle knives."

"Not yet," Thorn said. "No other injuries?"

"Signs of a struggle in each case, producing minor bruises and abrasions. Nothing that would kill, or even critically impair a healthy man from exercising self-defense."

"And yet."

"And yet." The doctor nodded, frowning. "They were seemingly *held down* somehow, while they were... killed."

"More than one person, then."

"I'd have to say so. Yes."

"I thank you for your time, Doctor. Where would I find your Mister Dickson, if I need to ask him anything?"

"Just opposite the livery," Baldridge replied. "He keeps his hearse and horses there."

Thorn was already turning toward the door, when Doctor Baldridge asked him, "Are you good with those six-guns?"

"I get along all right."

The medic nodded, then said, "Please be careful, anyhow."

Deputy Charley Kuhn tried acting casual, distracted, when the man in black—Gideon Thorn, apparently, if you could trust the hotel's register and what he'd told to Marshal Pike—stepped out onto the sidewalk from the doctor's office. Peering through the window of a shop that specialized in women's goods and sundries, Kuhn felt foolish, like a Peeping Tom so stupid that he couldn't wait for sundown. He'd been trailing Thorn and trying not to show it since the man in black finished his breakfast at McGuffy's, and before that he'd gone over every WANTED poster in the marshal's office, looking for a reason to arrest him.

Coming up with nothing.

Now he had a choice to make, as Thorn began to cross Sagrado Boulevard, apparently not seeing him, or else not letting on he did. Kuhn could pursue him, boost the odds of being spotted at it, or he could hang back and question Doctor Baldridge about what the stranger had discussed with him.

One prospect was about as welcome as the other, since the sawbones didn't seem to like him much. Kuhn had only the barest reason for that feeling, nothing in the way Baldridge had treated him or spoken to him on the one occasion Kuhn had seen him as a patient, for a bad chest cold, but rather something in the way the doctor looked at him, like there was some divide between them Kuhn could never bridge, no matter how he tried to put on airs.

And if he talked to Baldridge, would the doctor even tell him anything? Kuhn knew about the oath a sawbones took in school, named for a hippopotamus or some damn thing, swearing he wouldn't share a client's secrets, even if it came to life or death. If Thorn had gone to Baldridge as a patient, Kuhn would just be battering his head against a cold brick wall. But on the other hand, if Thorn was prying into other people's business for a "case," as he'd told Marshal Pike...well wasn't that fair game?

Before Kuhn finished pondering the point, his man was halfway down the thoroughfare, nearing the Free Will Church of God, where Reverend Alonzo Jefferson preached hellfire Sunday mornings and led earnest prayers on Wednesday nights. Kuhn didn't patronize the church, himself, viewing the whole thing as a waste of earthly time, tied up with schemes to pick his pocket for whatever he could spare when he was squeezed. Still, Preacher Jefferson knew damn near everyone in town and on the various surrounding farms to some extent, and God alone knew what salacious secrets he'd picked up from his parishioners.

Not who was killing folks and gutting them around the county, Kuhn supposed. Even a rock-ribbed minister would likely break his silence when it came to saving lives. And yet, Kuhn knew there were at least a couple of Sagrado residents who had their doubts about the reverend. He'd heard two of them talking, some time back, at Starbuck's, one man saying, "Who else you know that talks about openin' hearts and all?" To which the man's companion, nearly three sheets to the wind, had nodded thoughtfully and belched.

A preacher killing people sounded like a load of horse apples to Kuhn, but then he thought about John Brown, the damned fanatic who had killed all over Bleeding Kansas, then gone on to grab the arsenal at Harper's Ferry, in Virginia, where he lit a fuse that sparked the War Between the States.

People were goddamned strange, Kuhn thought, and looking worse to him the more he studied on it. Who could say what happened in Sagrado's homes, behind closed doors and shuttered windows, much less on the isolated farms where slaughter had become numbing routine?

Turning his full attention toward the Free Will Church of God, Kuhn saw the man in black outside it, hesitating for a moment on the steps, then going up to make his way inside. There was no way to trail him now, until he came back out, and in the meantime Kuhn decided that it wouldn't hurt to try the doctor, just in case.

EIGHT

Thorn was relieved to hear no bell announce his entry when he stepped into the Free Will Church of God. He didn't care much for the posturing of organized religion, but it struck him that a metal clanking sound each time the door swung to and fro would violate decorum even in the humblest of chapels.

It was cooler than the street, and definitely darker, as the church door closed behind him. Windows high up on the walls to either side admitted daylight that would stream above the heads of seated worshipers like something from an illustration in their Bible, and a stained glass image set above the pulpit seemed to show a bearded figure with his hands raised, but the workmanship was on the rough side—likely by some local, self-styled artisan—and Thorn couldn't have said for sure.

He stood in silence for a moment, taking in the atmosphere, before a stout man dressed much like himself —in black, minus the hat—emerged from somewhere back behind the pulpit, asking, "Can I help you, stranger?"

Thorn took off his hat, conscious as ever of the white

streak in his hair and the effect it had on some people, the first time that the saw it. "I've come looking for the minister," he said.

"And you have found him. Reverend Alonzo Jefferson. Who might you be, wearing a brace of pistols in the house of God?"

Thorn let that go and introduced himself. He didn't try to shake the preacher's hand, guessing that Jefferson was not in any mood for it. Instead, he started with a kind of lie, saying, "I was referred to you by Doctor Baldridge, up the street."

"In what capacity?"

"I'm looking into what's been happening around Sagrado in the past couple of months." Before the minister could answer back, he added, "That would be the murders."

"In what capacity? You don't appear to be a lawman, even with the guns."

"No, sir. As I've explained to Marshal Pike, I have an interest in matters of this kind, and some success in solving certain mysteries where the authorities have failed."

"When you say 'certain mysteries'..."

"Unusual and unexpected deaths. "

"And what is that experience?"

"I've brought more than my share of murderers to justice in Missouri, in Nevada, Texas and New Mexico."

"What kind of justice, may I ask?"

"Well, in Missouri, back nine months or so, the court hanged Roark Lindsay for devouring unfortunates he came across while traveling the countryside. That one was in the papers, if you care to read about it."

"And the others?"

"Some were written up, some not. I sense you're asking me if I'm a bounty hunter, and the answer would be 'no.' I take no pay from anyone, for anything I do. The understanding of it and protecting future victims is my sole reward."

"An altruist." Jefferson sounded skeptical.

"Hardly," Thorn said. "The answer lies in how I lost my family when I was young, and how I got this mark." He raised a hand to trace the white streak in his hair, adding, "But none of that concerns you, or Sagrado."

"So, what would you have from me?"

"I know you can't breach confidentiality with your parishioners, but you are in a place to notice any strange behavior, sudden changes in the way people behave, the attitudes they manifest. Before I start examining the crime scenes, I'd appreciate whatever I can get to point me on my way."

"And Marshal Pike approves of this?"

"He wished me luck," Thorn said, stretching the truth again. "I got the feeling he's done all he can."

"Well, Mr. Thorn, I might—just *might*—assist you if I could, but as it happens, I've been watching for the very things you mentioned, on my own, and I have nothing to report."

"I see. And nothing from your training as a minister suggests a motive for the kind of killing that's been going on?"

"The hearts, you mean."

"I do."

"You seem an educated man. I take it you're aware that human sacrifice, a blasphemy in thought and deed, has often stained the course of human history. We're told in Judges that the very children of Israel sacrificed their offspring to the false gods Ashtaroth and Baalim. I believe such practices continue to the present day among some heathen tribes around the world."

"But not in California?"

The preacher shrugged at that. "Where evil puts down roots, what man can say?"

Thorn saw that he was getting nowhere, thanked the minister, and turned to leave the church. Before he reached the door, Jefferson called out after him, "You're welcome back on Sunday, sir—without the guns."

"Let's see how that turns out," Thorn said, and passed into the morning sun.

Deputy Kuhn caught up with Marshal Pike as he was leaving a late breakfast at McGuffy's, probing at the molars on his lower right jaw with a toothpick. Charley let him finish, then began with, "So, I checked on Thorn with Arvid Chesney. He's the night man at the Easy Rest, and I asked him—"

"I know damn well who Chesney is," Pike interrupted him. "Get on with it."

"Okay. Short of it is, he swears Thorn didn't budge from the hotel all night."

"How sure is he?"

"Got testy when I asked him that, myself. Says he was wide-awake the whole night long and woulda heard Thorn, even if he tried a sneaker out the back. They got those stairs, you know, and—"

"Yeah. I've been inside the Easy Rest, Charley."

"Well, sure."

"So, barring somebody who contradicts Chesney, Thorn's not our man. Least not for last night's mess."

The pair of them had been called out before midnight, to look at Hayden Brokaw, or at what was left of him. To Charley Kuhn, he'd looked about the same as those who'd died before him, and it was a country mile from pretty, anyway you saw it. Letha Brokaw had been pretty much hysterical, which didn't help her young one, Danny. When the two of them had got there, summoned by a neighbor who'd been out late, setting traps for foxes, Letha had a big old pistol she was carrying around, as if the gun would do her any good.

Charley had stood around there, feeling useless, while the marshal questioned her as best he could, then grilled the neighbor—Hiram Danes—until Pike satisfied himself the man was innocent. From that point, there was nothing left to do but send the undertaker out with his assistant to retrieve the stiff for burial. They still had nothing on the stranger in their midst, damn it, and that meant they had nothing, period.

"Marshal, I don't see why we can't just—"

"Run 'im outa town? For one thing, Charley, it ain't *legal,* not least ways until he does somethin' to warrant it. And in the second place, I ain't entirely sure he'd listen to us, anyhow."

"Listen? Against the two of us with shotguns, should we need 'em?"

"Deputy, this ain't Dodge City, and it *certainly* ain't Tombstone. Thorn's an irritant right now, but nothin' more. And anyhow, I've started thinkin' that he might be useful to us, after all."

"Useful? How's that?" Kuhn asked.

"You grant that while he's askin' questions, he'll be stirrin' people up?"

"Hell, yeah. That's why—"

"Just let me finish, will ya? If he's stirrin' people up, odds are that one of 'em might make a slip."

"What kinda slip?"

"Maybe the kind a crazy killer makes, when he thinks someone's closin' in on 'im."

That took a minute sinking in, then Charley frowned and asked, "You're thinkin' someone here in town's behind the killins? Somebody we *know*?"

"Consider it," Pike said. "We've only got one stranger in Sagrado, just showed up, and now he's got an alibi for last night's crime from Arvid Chesney at the Easy Rest. Unless the night man has a change of heart, I guess we need to look at someone else."

"Well, Jesus, Orrin—I mean, Marshal. I don't like to think it's somebody we know and talk to ever day. I don't like that at all."

"I don't like anything about this whole thing, Charley. But if someone makes a try on Thorn to shut him up with all his questions...well, it might be good for us."

"Use him as bait, you mean?"

"Don't have to *use* him any way at all. Just let him do what he's already doin', keep an eye on 'im, and move right quick if somebody tries anything."

"Well, you can damn sure count on me, Marshal."

"I better had," Pike said. "It's what the county pays ya for."

Ujarak watched the man in black emerging from the Free Will Church of God and moving toward Sagrado's livery—or would it be the shop where white men took their dead for packaging before the put them in the ground? Such rituals were strange and foreign to Ujarak, who believed the dead should be returned to *ka'an*—what white men called the sky, or Heaven, in the smoke from blazing pyres. To place them in a box and bury them in filthy dirt offended him as sacrilege.

Ujarak's name translated roughly in the white man's tongue as "like a rock." It fit him well, since he was strong and steadfast in devotion to his people and their future in the land that once was theirs. Today, he had a relatively minor task assigned to him, but meant to carry out his duty without fail, watching the stranger as he moved around Sagrado, asking questions to the detriment of what was coming. What must be.

Ostensibly, Ujarak had been sent to buy supplies, and while he'd purchased some in fact—waiting his turn as white men pushed their way before him in the shops—his full attention had been focused on the man in black since he had left the Easy Rest Hotel, next ate his breakfast at McGuffy's, then began to circulate around the small, dry town, meeting first with the *ts'ats'aak*, their physician, and the shaman—*hmen*, in Ujarak's tongue—inside the white-washed church. Guiding his wagon slowly down Sagrado Boulevard, Ujarak waited now to see his subject's next stop and determine what he had in mind.

White people on the street ignored Ujarak for the most part. In their eyes, he was a simple Mexican who worked on one of the outlying farms to earn his meager keep. The few who thought they knew his name referred to him as Agustin Espina, although most would simply call him "boy" when speaking to his face. Although they lived on land stolen from Mexico, they viewed its rightful owners and inhabitants with high-minded disdain, convinced of their own God-granted superiority.

All that would change, and soon, but first, Ujarak had to do his part, discover what the man in black desired and what had brought him here, before he ruined anything.

Gossip had told Ujarak the man's name: Gideon Thorn. It meant nothing to him, but there was something in the stranger's face, his attitude, suggesting that he might be dangerous. The weapons that he carried did not faze Ujarak, common as they were among the white men, and completely useless if they sought to stop the stars in *ka'an* from following their course as prophesied. No, it was something in the tall man's eyes, the very way he moved, that told Ujarak he might have to be removed, and soon, in order for Kisin to be appeased.

Ujarak dared not make that move himself, without first speaking to Gabor, explaining what he'd seen and letting his anointed leader say what must be done. To strike without instructions might spoil everything and bring damnation down upon Ujarak's head. But still, as he'd passed by the stranger once that morning, touching-close but hardly noticed, it had take all Ujarak's self-control to keep from whipping out the knife he carried sheathed upon his belt and thrusting it between Thorn's ribs.

For just a heartbeat there, Ujarak had imagined hot blood spurting free onto his hand, then gushing to the wooden sidewalk, soaking instantly into its sagging, sun-bleached boards. Perhaps he had been smiling to himself, because Thorn glanced at him, as if from curiosity, before continuing along his way.

Ujarak knew he must exert more strength of will in future, keeping up what white men called a "poker face." In daily life, when forced to move among them, he was no one, less than nothing in their eyes. They must not ever see his power shining through, much less discover what it meant.

Flicking the wagon's reins lightly, Ujarak set it rolling slowly toward the livery and undertaker's parlor at the western edge of town, waiting to see which one the man in black would pick for his next stop.

Elmo Dickson was as advertised, the standard small-town undertaker dressed to suit his role. Standing inside the front room of the funeral parlor, matching Dickson's firm handshake, Thorn saw that there was little difference in how they dressed, though Dickson wore no hat indoors and was, of course, unarmed as far as Thorn could see.

"I've heard about you, Mr. Thorn," he said.

"News travels fast."

"Indeed it does. People don't know quite what to make of you. They're frightened, as I'm sure you understand, and any stranger in their midst right now causes more speculation than it might some other time."

"Well, if you get a chance to spread the word," Thorn said, "kindly assure them that I mean no harm to anyone—except the killer, if we happen to cross paths."

"It's being said that you investigate such matters privately," Dickson observed.

"That much is true. For some years now, I've traveled, looking into things the local law hasn't quite managed to explain. I fail sometimes, of course. In other cases, though, I've brought unfortunate events to a conclusion."

"How, if I may ask?"

"That all depends upon the circumstances," Thorn replied. "If I can find a person at the root of it, I'm happy to cooperate with law enforcement, if they're willing. Otherwise, I do what I think best. And if the problem's not of human origin..."

Thorn let it trail away, but Dickson jumped in, asking, "What does that mean?"

"In a couple of those situations, it turned out an animal was at the root of it. Another time, there was a man who only *thought* he was an animal." Thorn raised an index finger, tapped his temple with it, and concluded, "I've learned that the mind can do peculiar things."

"I won't dispute that," Dickson said, but offered no examples from his own experience. "What can I do for you, within the limits of propriety?"

"I've come from Dr. Baldridge," Thorn explained. "He said that in the victims he'd observed, the hearts were cut out of their bodies, not torn out by fang or claw."

"I must concur with his opinion."

"Nothing else about the victims indicated any other cause of death?

"Nothing at all."

"But there were superficial marks of struggle and restraint?"

"On arms and legs, primarily," Dickson agreed. "Some bruising on the face and ribs of two or three, as if they'd done some fighting back but got the worst of it and couldn't hold their own."

"No signs of any animal attack at all?"

"Oh, goodness, no. All six—well, make that seven, now—were killed at home, with family or friends nearby to watch over their last remains."

"So you would hold humans responsible."

The undertaker frowned. Replied, "If you could call them that, with the atrocities they have committed."

"Likely more than one, in fact?"

"From what I've seen, my educated guess would be a group of three or four, to overpower strapping men and pin their limbs while one...does what was done."

"Some kind of plan, then," Thorn surmised. "Not just a madman run amok."

"Unless they share the same insanity," Dickson replied. "But that seems almost laughable."

"Or maybe not as far-fetched as we think," Thorn said. He shook the undertaker's hand again and exited from Boot Hill's anteroom.

Despite the breakfast he'd consumed that morning, Thorn could feel his stomach rumbling, warning him of lunchtime's swift approach. McGuffy's was the only place for travelers to eat in town, but he'd not seen the limits of their menu yet, and started back in that direction, noticing the man who had to be a deputy of Marshal Pike across the thoroughfare, pretending not to watch Thorn's every move.

So be it. If the local law had nothing more to do than follow him around, Thorn was agreeable. So far, at least, he had nothing to hide.

Watching the deputy watch him, Thorn missed the woman stepping out into his path, nearly colliding with her, then recovering in time to touch one of her arms lightly and offer his apology.

"I must have been distracted, Ma'am. I hope you can forgive my clumsiness."

"Think nothing of it, Mr. Thorn," she said. "I thrive on taking people by surprise."

Thorn looked her over briefly: five foot five or six, face striking without any cosmetic enhancement, auburn hair drawn back into a bun that stopped just short of stark severity. Her body, clad in calico, with just a touch of lace around collar and cuffs, seemed slim and taut. How much of that she owed to whalebone stays was anybody's guess, and since she wore no wedding band, Thorn wondered if the mystery had ever been addressed.

"You know my name," he said, not asking her.

"I'd wager half the town, at least, knows who you are by now."

He smiled. "A name won't always tell you who a person is."

"And that's exactly why I hope to speak with you."

"Because...?"

"*My* name is Dinah Pilcher, editor and publisher of the *Sagrado Sentinel.* Since you've already set the town abuzz, I thought it might be nice to tell your story accurately, maybe put some worried minds at ease."

A newswoman. Thorn thought at once of Angelina Farnum, back in Texas, who had tried her best to cover his encounter with a creature from the vast abyss of time and managed to convince no one outside the mining town where those events had been played out, so many lives ended before the curtain fell.

"Well?" Dinah Pilcher prodded him. "What do you think?"

"Sorry. I got distracted for a second," Thorn replied. "You brought to mind a friend I used to have."

"Tell me about her over lunch," she said. "I'm buying. Then tell me what brings to Sagrado, Mr. Thorn."

NINE

McGuffy's waitress and his other diners all seemed more surprised than usual when Thorn walked in with Dinah Pilcher at his side. The waitress smiled as usual and welcomed both of them as if she really meant it, while the seated customers seemed torn between frowning at Gideon and fearing to insult their local newswoman. Thorn took advantage of the moment, grinned at all of them, and watched them turn away, embarrassed, as if he'd caught them at something.

"That was strange," Dinah remarked, when they were seated facing one another at the window table he'd begun to think of as his own.

"I get it every time I come here," Thorn replied. "They don't know what to make of you, right now."

"Oh, well. I'm bound to ruffle feathers," she replied. "Comes with the job."

The waitress took their orders, Thorn's for pulled-pork barbecue with fried potatoes on the side, Dinah's for a roasted chicken breast and greens. When she'd supplied their coffee, Dinah settled down to business, saying first,

"It's rude, I guess, but may I ask what happened to your hair?"

"No problem," Thorn replied. "It's from a childhood injury. I couldn't tell you why the hair turned white, but there's a scar beneath it, if you're close enough to see it."

"That sounds like a story in itself."

"Not one I lightly share."

"All right, then. How about what brings you to Sagrado in this season of our discontent?"

"You read Shakespeare, I take it."

"Whenever I have time. And my question?"

"You know why I'm here, or you wouldn't have stopped me outside."

"*Touché*. I know the 'what,' but not the 'why,' and while we're at it, I'd like to learn more about the 'who'."

Thorn scanned the dining room, spending a moment to collect his thoughts before he said, "The 'why' is in my blood, I guess. I travel as I'm able, following reports of mysteries I glean from newspapers or gossip on the road. Most often—though not always—they involve somebody getting killed in ways the local law can't understand."

"And you do?"

"Shouldn't you be taking notes?"

"No need." She raised an index finger to her temple. "I have what's called a photographic memory."

"Must get crowded in there."

"I'm getting by. My question?"

"Right. I don't know much of anything about a crime until I've looked at any evidence available. The difference, with me, is that I'm willing to consider options that a cop might not, because they're too ... unusual."

"Examples?"

"For the stranger ones, I'd have to let you speak with

someone else. Others who went through it along with me, so you don't think I'm spinning tales or just hallucinating."

"Who else would that be?"

"One might be Angelina Farnum. She's—"

"Like me," Dina chimed it. "She publishes *The Heiroglyph* in New Egypt, Texas." Seeing his look of mild surprise, she said, "There aren't that many of us, Mr. Thorn. We like to keep in touch."

"So write and ask about my visit there, last year. I'll let her tell you whatever she wants to say."

"No hints? No clues?"

"I wouldn't want to put words in her mouth."

"Very mysterious, I must say."

"That's a problem with the so-called unbelievable. Even when someone knows the truth, selling it to the world is something else again."

"I *will* write to her. If you're bluffing—"

"Not my style," he told her, as he saw the waitress bustling toward them with their meals.

Marshal Pike couldn't help frowning as he saw Gideon Thorn and Dinah Pilcher walk into McGuffy's, not quite arm-in-arm, but close enough to tell him they were getting on the friendly side. He'd looked askance at journalists throughout his whole life as a lawman, but in this case, if he focused hard enough, Pike thought there just might be an up side to the thing, as well. With any luck, the lady editor might pry some secrets out of Thorn and publish them, help Pike find out what he was really doing in Sagrado—and, if she was harsh enough, maybe encourage Thorn to head on out of town.

Or maybe she was drawn to him by his appearance and what some might call his charm. Pike granted that the young man wasn't bad to look at, once you got around the freakish white streak on his scalp, but looking pretty on the outside didn't mean he could be trusted, much less that he wouldn't make things worse around Sagrado, accidentally or otherwise.

Pike turned away and scanned the thoroughfare, seeking his deputy. He'd sent Kuhn off to question anyone they knew that Thorn had spoken to so far, which meant the sawbones, Preacher Jefferson, and Elmo Dickson at the undertaker's parlor. Charley should be back before much longer, and while Pike expected nothing in the way of epic revelations, he was hoping Thorn had dropped a hint or two about how he planned to approach the murders, even solve them if the opportunity arose.

And wouldn't that make Pike look like a puredee fool, the way he'd fumbled, finding nothing in the way of evidence, before a total stranger wandered in and raised the veil? It might not be enough to get him voted out of office at the next election, but it wouldn't help his chances, either.

But would giving up the job, even his place in the community, be all that bad?

He had been feeling stale for months now, wasted in a post that offered him no situations that surprised or stimulated him, no prospect for advancement. Then again, at Pike's age, with the small amount of money he had laid by in Sagrado's Savings Bank and Trust, what else could he expect? Whatever shot he'd had at greatness had been spent and left behind him long ago. By any calculation, he had peaked before he landed in Sagrado, and the rest of it was all downhill from there.

He spotted Charley coming up the street and raised a

hand in greeting, waited while his deputy crossed over and approached him at a trot. When he was close enough to hear without Pike shouting out, the marshal asked, "Well? Anything?"

Kuhn slowed down to a walk and joined him on the shaded sidewalk. "Well, he met all three of 'em, just like I said. They claim he didn't tell 'em anything, just asked 'em questions and moved on."

"What kinda questions?"

"With Doc Baldridge and Elmo, he mostly asked about the wounds, you know. How was the hearts removed, like, whether someone cut 'em or just tore 'em out."

"He's ruling out an animal."

"Say what?"

"Nothin'. Go on."

"Now, with the reverend, he took another tack. Tried askin' 'im if he knew anyone in town who mighta done somethin' like this."

"I'm guessing Pastor Jefferson said no."

Kuhn bobbed his head. "Told me same thing he told the stranger, that he's all for bein' confident—"

"You mean, for confidentiality?"

"That's it, all right. But if he knew someone was doin' crimes, he'd turn 'em in under the law."

"So, we know nothin' more than yesterday."

"Well, no. I guess not. Where's he at right now?"

"Talkin' to Dina Pilcher, over to McGuffy's."

"What the hell?"

Pike frowned again and said, "I guess we'll have to wait and see."

"I read about the Lindsays in Missouri," Dinah said. "They carried something in the *Liberty Tribune*, claiming they were a tribe of cannibals."

"That sums it up," Thorn said, taking another bite of spicy pork.

"And *you* caught them?"

"Well, it was touch and go there, for a while. Some of them didn't want to come along."

"And you..."

"Shot them," he said. "Kept them from chowing down on me."

"The law must have been grateful for your help."

"Sure. They were kind enough to give me good directions, heading out of town."

"But why?"

"Same reason that your Marshal Pike won't take it kindly if I catch a break and find out who's been killing farmers around here. It makes him look bad, and I don't expect the county sheriff will be tickled, either."

"I can help with that. I mean, if you're successful. Otherwise..."

"Then all you've got is some guy passing through. Nothing to help you sell a paper, right?"

"Sounds like the truth."

"In which case, why waste time checking my references? Each new case is a job unto itself. I can't promise results, or what they'll be if I discover something. There's nothing to see, till it's all said and done. Maybe not even then."

She took a bite of chicken, swallowed it, then said, "All right. Give me some background, then. Where do you come from? Who's your family? You strike me as an educated man, so—"

Thorn smiled, told her, "I should be, after Harvard."

"Harvard *University*?"

"The very same. Class of Seventy-three."

"And since then, you've been...traveling?"

"That's it. No family alive to tie me down."

"And this is your...vocation? Your calling?"

"I didn't hear a voice from Heaven, if that's what you mean. It goes back to my childhood."

"And the scar that you don't talk about?"

"Maybe another time. I'd have to know you better, and decide if it's something I wanted you to publish."

"Will you be around that long?" she asked.

"I never know. Sometimes I get a break right off. With this, I haven't even visited the crime scenes yet."

"You might want to be careful, doing that."

"And try not to get shot?"

"People are in a fighting mood. I grant you that."

"I'll watch my step."

"And keep me posted, if you please?"

He shrugged. "So far, I'd bet you know as much as I do, likely more. You may have known the victims, for example, when they were alive."

"Sadly, I can't say that I did. Sagrado's small, but not *that* small. The farmers come to town for church, on market days, but that's about the size of it."

"But now they matter," Thorn suggested. "Not just to the law, but to whoever's killing them."

"And what does that mean?"

"That," he answered, "is what I need to find out."

Ujarak saw the lookouts posted when he was a quarter-mile out from the farm. He did not slow or signal them in any way, in case there might be other, hostile eyes watching, and it was the lookouts' job to see if he was followed from Sagrado back to where the white men thought he lived. To the whites, he was a peasant, simple and dull-witted, but they might still grow suspicious of him as the homicides continued and the men with shiny stars proved helpless in preventing them.

As he approached the farm, Ujarak slowed his pace, waiting to see who would come out and greet him, seeking any information he had managed to collect in town. To his surprise, Gabor was waiting on the porch himself, with Cadmael beside him, both in straw hats that cast shade across their faces. Both of them, like Ujarak, were dressed as if to work the land, although they had tilled no soil since arriving, sowed no seeds, and were expecting no crop in the fall.

In fact, when fall came—if it came—they would be living in a different world.

"*Ola,*" Gabor called out to Ujarak when he had stopped the wagon's team. Two other men, dressed more or less the same, appeared from somewhere at the east side of the house and started to unload the various supplies he'd bought in town.

They lived simply, but had to eat in spite of everything. The load included corn, beans, flour and rice, along with simple tools they would not use, but which maintained the fiction of their presence on the farm. Its former owners had gone missing months ago, leaving no family to claim the place, and the bank in town had readily accepted Gabor's modest offer for the spread, despite the fact that he was Mexican.

Or, so the white men thought.

"*Qué aprendiste?*" Gabor asked, switching to common Spanish from the Old Tongue, out of habit from maintaining character. "What have you learned?"

"I saw the stranger all in black," Ujarak said, as he dismounted from the wagon's seat, leaving its reins to trail upon the ground. "He is a young man, well armed, with an air of danger, though he does not seem to threaten anyone."

"*A quién está visitando?*" asked their shaman. "Who is he visiting."

"The doctor, the *ministro,* and the town's *enterrador*, the tender of their dead."

"And no one else?"

"Not while I followed him. Of course, he came to town last night and may have spoken to the lawmen. I suppose as much, but cannot say with certainty."

"And he is here because of us." This time, when Gabor spoke, it did not strike Ujarak as a question.

Still, he answered back, "So says the gossip in the stores I visited. The shopkeepers regard him with suspicion, more than hope that he can help relieve them of their fear."

The shaman smiled at that. "Of course. He is too late to save them, even if he had the power—which no white man has. Who dares to stand before Kisin?"

The question was rhetorical. All present bowed their heads and muttered prayers to Kisin, asking for his blessing on their enterprise. When they were done, eyes raised once more, Gabor spoke for the lot of them. "His will be done!"

They were on second mugs of coffee, with their cleaned

plates cleared away, when Dinah asked Thorn, "How long do you plan to stay? I mean, what's usual?"

"Sorry. There is no 'usual' to what I do. Some jobs, I look around and finish in a day or so, if I decide there's nothing I can do. On others...well, events develop and I have to go along with them, or sometimes try my best to head them off. I don't have any schedule or rules."

"You come well armed, though," she observed.

"That's just as much for trouble on the trail, as anything. I can't predict ahead of time when force may need to be applied."

"But you don't stint from it."

"Confronted with a man or something else that means to kill you, heistation is the next best thing to suicide."

She frowned and said, "If I may ask you this, how many people have you killed."

Thorn's frown matched hers. "I don't keep score," he said. "No one who wasn't trying to harm me or someone under my protection. I can tell you I've got nothing on that Hank McCarty fellow in New Mexico, or Holliday, the dentist up in Arizona."

"So, you're not a gunfighter, per se."

"I wear guns, and I've fought with them. But no one hires me, and I wouldn't take a killing job for pay, regardless of the price."

"A man of principle."

"I like to think so, but the principles are mine. They may or may not satisfy society."

"All right. What's next for you, here in Sagrado. Questioning more townsfolk?"

"I suppose I'll have a look around as many murder scenes as might be feasible. I naturally hate to bother people when they're mourning, but the more time slips away, the cloudier their memories become, assuming they saw anything at all."

"What do you think about the boy, Enzo Velasquez, and his story of the giant birds?"

"I'm not equipped to say. If I can speak to him, it may be helpful. As we sit here, I can't tell you what he saw, if anything."

"But giant *birds*?"

"On that, I should refer you back to Angelina Farnum in New Egypt. What we worked on there was...similar, if not identical."

"I'll get a message in the post to her this afternoon," Dinah replied. "If you need help finding the farms where people lost their lives, or introductions to their families..."

"I'd better handle that alone. It has a certain risk, I know, but if they think I'm hooked up to the newspaper somehow, they might..."

"Think you were trying to exploit their stories?"

"Or that *you* were, dragging me along for company."

"I'm not sure whether I should be insulted, Mr. Thorn." But there were still the traces of a smile around the corners of her mouth, and in her eyes.

"I meant you no offense, Ma'am. Just stating the obvious."

"If you're not trying to offend me, how about you drop the 'Ma'am' and call me Dinah?"

"It's a deal," he said. "I'm Gideon, to friends."

"Well, Gideon, I think we'd better leave before my fellow residents start cooking up fresh gossip focused on the two of us."

Rising, and moving to draw back her chair, he said, "I'm used to it. No reputation to protect in the community."

"Some of the letters I get at the *Sentinel*, I'm not sure I've got any reputation left to save."

"Hate mail?" he asked her, as they started for the door.

"Let's say I have a few dependable subscribers who don't think a woman should be selling papers, much less writing what's contained in them. And they aren't shy about expressing their opinions."

"Maybe whatever you write, from what we've talked about, will pacify the town a little, anyway."

"I guess we'll see," she said, and shook Thorn's hand again before he turned away and started toward the livery.

TEN

Justice of the peace Julian Engle was a sixty-year-old man who could have passed for seventy, portly, with thinning snow-white hair and a bushy mustache to match. If dressed appropriately, he could probably have been mistaken for a southern planter from the years before the Civil War, but in the three-piece suit he wore to work, vest buttons straining to contain his girth, he looked more like his actual profession, as a lawyer slightly gone to seed.

The smell of Engle's rank cigar pervaded every corner of his office as he peered at Marshal Pike through swirling smoke, seated across the desk where Engle spent the better part of each weekday.

"So, what about this stranger then, Orrin?" he asked, his voice a growl that could turn menacing before defendants in his court.

"I spoke with 'im," Pike said, "and Charley's got an eye on 'im."

"Charley!" The judge snorted derisively. "Think he can find his own fly in a pinch?"

"He does awright, Judge. Anyhow, the stranger's done

nothin' to speak of, side from wanderin' around and askin' questions here in town so far."

"What questions?"

"Charley's lookin' into that, as well."

"Doing two things at once? I do declare, that boy's a wonderment." He blew more smoke, then asked, "And who's this Mister Thorn been talking to, so far?"

"About who you'd expect. The doctor, undertaker, and the preacher."

"Jefferson? That windbag? What in hell's he know about the killings?"

Pike shrugged. Said, "He prob'ly reckons Satan did it. You know him."

"I do, indeed."

"And one more person, Judge. Thorn had a long talk over lunch with Dinah Pilcher, at McGuffy's."

"Damn that meddling female!"

"I dunno," Pike said. "She's coverin' the crimes already. Only natural she'd wanna talk to him, when everybody else in town's been gossipin' since he rode in."

"Their gossip's one thing. Putting it black and white, where it might be picked up by newspapers that matter, *that* is something else entirely."

"Well, there's nothin' I can do about it anyhow," Pike said. "She'd just start yellin' 'freedom of the press' or some such thing, and if it went to court, you'd wind up sidin' with her."

Engle shook his head. Said, "Orrin, sometimes I despair of you. *Of course*, I'd have to side with her in court. We've got the goddamned First Amendment to the U.S. Constitution saying she can print most anything she wants to. There's no changing that...under the law."

"Whatever that means."

"You know damn well what it means. There's ways and ways of stopping someone when they're doing something you don't like, that causes damage to the whole community at large. We talked about this early on, when she questioning the county sheriff's way of dealing with stray Mexicans."

Pike shifted in his chair, sat up a little straighter as he faced Engle. "And what I told you then," he said, "still goes. As long as I'm wearin' a badge, I won't do anything against the law. No way."

"And if some other restless souls were less inclined to follow all the niceties? Would you feel duty-bound to lock 'em up?"

"I would."

"Well, then." The judge sat back and raised his hands, a gesture some might have mistaken for defeat. "There's nothing more to say about the subject, I suppose. Go on and do your duty as you see it, Orrin. Where the stranger is concerned, I hope you'll take a dim view of him bothering the recently bereaved."

Pike rose and said, "If any of 'em brings me a complaint, you bet I'll act on it. Outside a town, though, as you realize, I've got no jurisdiction to be trailin' 'im around and seein' where he goes or who he talks to."

"No, quite right," the judge said, nodding. "Everyone is free to move around and talk, as they see fit. Let's hope and pray that nothing happens to him, out there on the range."

"If you've got somethin' cookin', Julian, you'd better let me know right now."

"Don't get yourself riled up, Marshal. I wouldn't lift a finger against Mister Thorn. That's strictly your department, should the need arise."

Scowling, Pike turned and left the office without bothering to close the door.

Thorn stepped into the livery's shade and waited for the hostler, busy shifting heavy bags of oats, to notice him. After they'd said "hello," he went to check on Bell and found her reasonably happy in her clean stall, munching feed. They spent a moment, silently exchanging thoughts, while Thorn reached in to scratch behind Bell's ears. As far as he could tell, she felt all right and was content to stay a while.

Shadow, for his part, let Thorn know that he was ready for a run. "We're going," Thorn assured him, as he led the gray out of his stall and set about the task of saddling him, telling the hostler that he'd see to it himself.

When he had the stallion saddled up, Thorn thanked the hostler for the care he'd given both his animals so far. He rode back to the Easy Rest and went upstairs, causing the clerk to hike his eyebrows when Thorn came back down with Winchester in hand. To throw him off, Thorn said, "A little hunting trip," and hit the sidewalk smiling, sheathed the rifle in its saddle boot, and mounted up again.

He had directions to the Brokaw spread, scene of the most recent attack, and was informed that Hayden Brokaw left a widow and one child, a boy of ten years old. Disturbing them—or any of the other victims' families—would not have been Thorn's first choice, but he'd gone as far as he could manage with Sagrado's townsfolk. It was time to look around the murder scenes, see what was left after the killers fled with human hearts torn from their prey. Thorn had no preconceptions as to what he might expect, but knew the fresher scenes. Brokaw's and Austin Lovett's farms, held the most promise for surviving clues.

As he was riding out of town, Thorn caught the marshal's deputy observing him without much subtlety. He knew the lawmen's jurisdiction should be bounded by Sagrado's town limits, but Thorn had also worked in places where the law was commonly ignored, particularly when a nosy stranger was involved. He'd watch for shadows on the trail, but didn't plan on starting any confrontations with a man wearing a star.

So far, they had no legal cause to run him out of town, but that could change immediately if Thorn pushed the marshal or his deputy too far.

Thorn liked the open country, always had, a welcome change from Boston's crowded streets, its busy ports and stinking factories. Thorn hadn't visited the manse on Beacon Hill in nearly two years now, and couldn't rightly say he missed it, though he *did* miss spending time with his old friend, Obi Magoro. They still kept in touch through telegrams and letters, when Thorn had the time to write, but he shared little of his strange adventures in the West.

Some things, he'd learned, where best not put on paper for posterity.

If he'd written about the Texas dragon, for example, or the mountain devils he had faced to save a logging camp in northern California, a stranger reading it would instantly concluded Thorn was insane. Same with the ghost town that had nearly claimed his life in Kansas, until Thorn managed to burn most of it down.

Those aspects of his life were unbelievable to most, the people who had never witnessed anything outside the norm and felt their worlds turned upside-down by doubt of all that civilized society maintained was true. Thorn's mind had opened further from the time when he was orphaned, at the tender age of two, and he'd learned more from Aunt Drusilla of the occult sciences and what she called the Other Side, as he grew up under her stately roof and she put him through Boston's finest schools.

Drusilla had been strange, but masked it well behind her wealth and status in Brahmin society. When she consorted with Paschal Beverly Randolph, the mixed-race physician, occultist, Spiritualist, trance medium, and writer, no one in Drusilla's inner circle said a word against her, captivated as they all were by the latest fads in mysticism and the aura of Thorn riches at Drusilla's fingertips. Randolph had died last year, under disputed circumstances in Ohio, at the age of forty-nine. Drusilla had preceded him across the bridge of death, but Gideon could still recall the sittings and séances they had held on Beacon Hill, attended by some of the richest people in New England's Cradle of Liberty.

What would Drusilla and the others think about him now?

No matter. Gideon had charted his own course, and on this sunny afternoon, it led him toward another scene of death.

Deputy Kuhn saw Thorn ride out of town and knew he should report that news to Marshal Pike without delay, but Pike was in with Judge Engel just then, and barging in on Engle was like throwing pebbles at a hungry bear. Engle had no great love for Kuhn—in fact, Charley believed the fat man hated him—and he would not invite another of the paunchy jurist's tongue-lashings for no good reason, when the word of Thorn's departure from Sagrado could be saved for later on.

Charley began to wonder about that, though, when he spotted Dinah Pilcher riding out of town on her bay mare, a few short minutes after Thorn and headed in the same direction. Kuhn put two and two together, didn't like the answer he came up with, but then had to stop and wonder. If the lady editor was working with the man in black on whatever in hell he hoped to do, why didn't they ride out together in the first place?

No. It felt more as if she was following the drifter, without wanting him to catch her at it. Sneaky like, and what in hell was up with that?

Okay, a mystery, which might peak Orrin's interest, but then Kuhn thought about Judge Engle's scowling countenance and put the whole thing back on hold. Wherever Thorn and his shadow were headed, it was out of town, and that meant well beyond the bounds of Pike's authority. The law might let him chase a bandit, say, if Pike had seen him rob a downtown store, but any vague investigation in the hinterlands fell under jurisdiction of the sheriff's office, and old Sheriff Bubba Coleman wasn't seeing eye to eye with Orrin on the murders. Coleman blamed a gang of outlaws up from Mexico and didn't puzzle much over the missing hearts, just calling it a "greaser deal" and dropping it at that.

Pike figured Bubba had it wrong, and wasn't shy of saying so, which put the sheriff off and had him cussing underneath his breath the last time he had left Sagrado. Neither one of them would yield, and since Kuhn drew his pay from Orrin Pike, it wouldn't do for him to back the other side, particularly when he didn't have a damned idea, himself, as to what lay behind the killings.

Charley took a quick look at his watch, decided Orrin should be finished with Judge Engle by the time he reached the old man's office, boot heels clomping on the dusty sidewalk as he went.

Dina Pilcher caught Deputy Kuhn eyeballing her as she rode out of town on Vixen, her bay mare, and sent a careless smile in his direction while she cursed him silently for being such a snoop.

"Like I should talk," she told Vixen, "when snooping's all I do."

It was her job, of course, to unearth news and keep Sagrado's townspeople informed of what was going on around them, both within their county and across the world. Because of her opinions on such things as women's suffrage, January's order sending all surviving Indians to reservations, the Whiskey Ring in Washington, and the accelerating presidential race that threatened to dismantle Reconstruction, she had drawn her share of flack from readers—and from some she guessed could barely read at all, like the pathetic rubes who'd smeared her office windows with horse dung two months ago.

"The price of fame," she said, and laughed as she crossed over the town limits, trailing Gideon Thorn toward the late Brokaw spread. She hoped he wouldn't catch her at it—not, at least, until she meant him to.

She knew how these things worked. A husband died, leaving his wife and children on the land alone. Most often, the survivors pulled up stakes and left to live with family or find work in a city. Otherwise, the widow could employ farmhands, if she had any cash in hand, and thus spawn rumors, usually spread by local farmers hoping they could pick her land up on the cheap.

All boys together, trying in their not-so-subtle ways to keep women under their thumbs.

In a nutshell, she supposed that was the reason why some people seemed to hate her. Dinah dared to voice her own opinions and to challenge theirs—a sin, in some men's eyes, against the very laws of Nature.

Most men, but seemingly, not Gideon Thorn.

He had a shady past and liked to keep it hidden, but Dinah had sensed no kind of prejudice while they were talking on the street, or at McGuffy's restaurant. He didn't try to brush her off or lord it over her, as if she were a simple-minded fool to have opinions or inquire into his business in Sagrado.

Granted, when she heard his explanation, it was...strange, to say the least. He kept allusions to his other cases vague in the extreme, but Dinah definitely planned to get in touch with Angelina Farnum at the *Heiroglyph* and see what she could learn about the time Thorn spent with her.

"A man of mystery," she told Vixen, watching the trail ahead for any sign of Gideon. "That's not all bad, I guess."

She didn't want to overtake him on the road and make a scene. The way she'd planned it, if they just showed up at Hayden Brokaw's place, a few minutes apart, she could excuse it as coincidence, a follow-up, perhaps even inspired by lunch with Gideon. From there...well, if they wound up working on the case together, that was fine with her. If he still balked, Dinah would do what she had always done in journalism and her life at large: go it alone.

"That doesn't mean I'm lonely," she observed, while

Vixen paid no heed. "I'm *independent,* damn it! There's a major difference, all right?"

Above her, barely visible, a solitary vulture wheeled among sparse clouds, its sharp eyes doubtless scouring the earth below for its next meal. She wondered if it was an omen, then rebuked herself for giving in to childish superstition.

Still, she couldn't help but think that there was more death on the way.

ELEVEN

The Brokaw spread felt lifeless, even with a crowd of chickens strutting in the yard and pecking scattered feed, hogs rooting in a nearby pen. A lowing from inside the barn told Thorn there was at least one cow in residence, as well. His mind reached out to calm the animals, both seen and hidden from his view, but Thorn's strange talent didn't work on humans, and he knew he'd have to watch his step as he approached the house, reining his stallion to a walking pace and eyeing window shutters that seemed tightly closed.

His first guess was that Brokaw's widow and their son had left the place, still traumatized by Hayden's recent death and fearful of remaining on the property alone. A second, closer look showed Thorn a buckboard parked around beside the barn, half out of sight, its tongue and traces trailing on the ground. He knew the widow and her child might have departed from the spread by other means, but that seemed less than likely.

Thorn was just about to call out toward the farmhouse when its front door opened and a haggard-looking woman stepped onto the porch. Her eyes were red from weeping, and he might have called her hair unkempt, but he was focused on the shotgun in her hands.

"That's far enough," she cautioned him. "Don't fool yourself to thinking I can't drop you where you sit."

"No need for that, Ma'am," Thorn replied. "I mean you and your boy no harm."

His mention of the child, presumably still hiding somewhere in the house, produced no softening of Widow Brokaw's features or expression; quite the opposite, in fact. Her lips compressed into a narrow line, as if someone had carved them with a razor and a steady hand. She cocked one of the shotgun's hammers, and its double barrels swung around toward Thorn.

"I don't know you," she said, "but I can think of half a dozen reasons why a stranger might come out here, knowin' that my husband's crossed the river. None of the ones that come to mind are good. You've got one minute, Mister. Either speak your piece or turn around and ride away while you still can."

Thorn knew she meant it. Even though she'd likely never shot a man before, her tragedy had pushed her to the edge and she might blast him from his saddle on a whim, unless he made his case directly and in haste.

"You've got nothing to fear from me," Thorn told her, hearing how hollow it sounded the moment he spoke. "My name's Gideon Thorn, and I'm new in Sagrado. I came because I heard about the killings, hoping I can stop them."

"What business is that of yours?" she challenged. "I don't see a badge, and you don't look like any lawman that I ever saw."

"No, Ma'am. Truth is, I look into these things because of something that destroyed my family when I was just a kid, younger than yours. I haven't found the answer for it yet, but I have managed to prevent some other wicked things from happening."

"Like what?" she asked him, narrow-eyed.

"There have been other murders," Thorn replied. "None like what's happened here, but others just as bad, some even worse. I've helped to apprehend the killers in about ten cases I can think of, right off hand."

"What happened to 'em?"

"Most of them are dead. One's locked in an asylum, won't be getting out."

She seemed about to ask him something else, then looked past Thorn and snapped, "Now, who's that you brought with you?"

"With me? Ma'am, I came alone."

"So, who's *that,* then?"

Thorn swiveled slowly in his saddle, hands clear of his holstered guns, and saw another rider drawing closer. Sixty yards and closing, recognition hit him, but the Widow Brokaw got there first. "Is that Miz Pilcher from the newspaper in town?"

"Looks like it," Thorn replied. "I promise you, she didn't ride along with me."

A moment later, Pilcher was beside him, seated on a young bay mare. "What are you doing here?" he asked.

"Free country, last I checked," she said, smiling. "And hey, I might keep you from getting shot."

Dinah Pilcher saw that Thorn was irritated, but she didn't let it bother her. Most men whom she dealt with on any given day were irritated about something that she'd written or had failed to write about, her views on this or that subject, often the very fact that any woman claimed the right to have opinions and express them publicly. She wanted Gideon to like her, for some reason that she didn't fully grasp as yet, but gathering the news came first.

"I don't think Mrs. Brokaw was about to shoot me," Thorn declared.

"You never know," the widow chimed in. "I just might've, given what's been going on around these parts."

Thorn turned to face the porch again, saying, "I'd rather that you didn't, Ma'am. I only hope to ask some questions that may help me get inside the killer's mind."

"I'd like to put a bullet in his so-called mind," the stricken farm wife answered back. "But now you're here, the two of you, you might as well come in and sit a spell."

Dinah flashed Thorn a sidelong smile, dismounted, and secured her mare's reins to a handrail on the porch. Thorn climbed down after her and did the same, a tinge of color in his cheeks suggesting—what? Embarrassment? Chagrin? Perhaps the faintest twinge of pleasure that she'd followed him?

Don't get distracted, Dinah told herself, as she retrieved her notepad and a pencil from her saddlebag. She followed Letha Brokaw back inside the silent house, Thorn on her heels. Inside, she saw the woman's son, now fatherless, watching with vacant eyes from what she guessed must be a bedroom doorway.

"Danny, just go back to sleep now," said his mother. "Close the door and get whatever rest you can."

"Yes'm," the boy replied, and disappeared from view.

They sat around a homemade dining table, thanking Letha for the fresh-made coffee she poured into metal cups. "I've got no cream," she said, "but sugar's on the table, if you want it." When they'd both sipped coffee and pronounced it good, she pressed ahead. "Now what about these questions? Are they for the *Sentinel*?"

"Mine aren't," Thorn said. "I can't speak for Miss Pilcher, here."

Her turn. "I'm covering what's happened to your family, of course," she said, "as with the other crimes around Sagrado during recent weeks."

"There isn't much to tell," Letha replied, fighting a tremor in her voice. "I didn't see what happened, nor did Danny. Hayden went out to see what had the hogs stirred up and making noise. He took a rifle with him, said he'd be back in a minute. Next thing that I hear's a shot, and then this...screaming. I had Danny here inside to think of, and...I swear, it felt like I was paralyzed. All I could do to walk across and bar the door."

The tears came then, full force, as Letha Brokaw hung her head, slim shoulders heaving with her sobs. "I left Hayden alone out there to die, goddamn my soul."

Dinah got up and went to her, holding her close, while Thorn's expression told her that he wished he were a thousand miles away from all that misery. "It's not your fault," she told the sobbing widow. "What could you have done outside but risk your own life, maybe leave your son alone and helpless?"

"But...but I..."

"But nothing," Dinah cut her off. "You did the only proper, mindful thing. Just think. Even if you'd rushed out the very second that you heard the shot, what could you possibly have changed? Their work was done by then, and you—"

The widow raised her head and interrupted. "They? You

said *their* work. You think there's more than one man mixed up in this thing?"

"It looks like three, at least," Thorn said. "To hold a man your husband's size and...well, do what was done."

Dinah could feel the widow trembling now, but not from crying. When she spoke, it sounded more like pent-up rage. "Three monsters, maybe more? What kind of people would do anything like this? The law's already said they don't blame Indians. What's left, then, when they sneak in here by night to kill, don't even bother stealing anything?"

"That's what I hope to learn," Thorn said, as if to both of them. "And when I know, then find a way to stop it happening again."

The watcher, known as Caprakan among his brothers, Angelo Martinez to the whites in town, was careful not to show himself, even as a dark speck against the open skyline. It meant life and death for him to carry out his mission at the farm—indeed, it might mean even more than that.

Gabor had given him the job to watch and see who visited the family of their most recent prey, observe whether the man's survivors left the property, if lawmen came and went, whatever might be helpful in the days ahead, before their goal was realized. Beyond that moment, nothing any white man did would matter in the fires and turmoil of a world reborn.

Caprakan had never seen the man in black before, but recognized him easily from Ujarak's description to the rest of them. As for the woman who had followed him, albeit at a cautious distance, she was someone Caprakan had seen around Sagrado when he joined in their supply runs to the small town—soon to be the epicenter of a great apocalypse. He thought she ran the local newspaper, but was not sure and did not really care.

Nothing the whites could say or print on paper would forestall the judgment that awaited them when Kisin came into his glory at long last. Those who supported and enabled Him would reap their just reward, while those who had opposed Him or stood watching from the sidelines like a flock of stupid sheep would all be swept away.

Lu'um, the Earth, reborn anew at last.

It was a signal honor for Caprakan to be one of those selected to initiate the final phase of such a monumental change, a great Awakening which would at once purge all polluted lands of their accumulated filth, and set the One True People back in the position they deserved, as kings and rulers of the world.

Caprakan watched the black-clad man approach the house on horseback, stopping when a woman with a long gun in her hands emerged. They talked a while, seeming at odds, before another rider came into the farmyard. This one, Caprakan discovered, was a woman. She exchanged words with the man in black, then said something that seemed to calm the farmer's widow on the porch. Eventually, both riders dismounted, tied their horses to the porch rail, and proceeded on inside the house.

The spy considered waiting, watching to determine when the visitors departed, but the afternoon was getting on, and he decided it would be a waste of time. Gabor would wish to know what he had seen, without the story's obvious conclusion that the visitors departed, riding back to town.

And where else would they go, with dusk impending now?

Caprakan wriggled down the backside of the rise that sheltered him, retrieved his horse, and set off for the farm his brothers occupied. He had fulfilled his duty for the moment, and with any luck, would be included on the next hunt when Gabor determined it was time.

They left the Brokaw home, if such it could be called today, with little more knowledge than they'd possessed upon arrival. Letha—through her tears, dead-eyed—had told them all she'd heard the night before, but having seen nothing herself, besides her husband's ravaged body, it shed no light on the mystery. Now, with the warm sun in the west and lowering, Thorn wondered if the afternoon had been a waste.

"Where to?" asked Dinah, when they'd put the house of pain behind them.

"How far to the next farm, Austin Lovett's?" Thorn inquired.

"I'd call it six or seven miles."

He read the sky and told her, "We'd be coming in at dusk. More likely to be shot that way."

"There hasn't been a case so far of killers striking twice in the same place," she said.

"You want to bet your life that someone nervous won't be standing watch?"

"Good point. So, back to town?"

"I guess so. By the time we drop the horses at the livery, it should be getting on toward supper time."

"I'd rather not start any more wild speculation at McGuffy's."

Surprised, and then embarrassed, Thorn could feel his neck flush, color creeping toward his cheeks. "I didn't mean—"

"But how about my house?"

"Your house?"

"Oh, did you think I had a rented room? Landlady peering down her nose and saying, 'No man under my roof after six o'clock'?"

"I hadn't thought—"

"So, what about it? I *can* cook, in case you're wondering. And not too badly, if I do say so myself."

"It feels like an intrusion," Thorn said, not quite stammering.

"If you're invited?"

"No. Of course, not."

"Well, then?"

"It would be my pleasure," he replied, a bit surprised to find he meant it.

"Good. That's settled, then. And you can tell me more about yourself, what set you on this quest of yours."

So that was it. Thorn felt himself relax a bit, as they returned to more familiar ground. He was not wholly inexperienced with woman. Was there any Harvard man who graduated clinging to his frail virginity? And since there were no women in the Harvard student body, that meant visiting a brothel or some hectic fumbling with a wayward debutante. So, Thorn had "been around," by standards of the time and place, but rarely had availed himself of any opportunities he found in western towns during his grim pursuit of the unknown. One didn't seem to fit the other, and the path he'd chosen had not proved conducive to romance.

But this, with Dinah Pilcher, should be safe enough, the thought. She was a businesswoman, a professional, who wanted information from him, for her newspaper. There was no reason to suspect a physical attraction on her part, even if Thorn found her alluring, and her open manner of expression sometimes verging on provocative.

With supper plans decided, they rode on in silence for a while, then Dinah asked, "Would you be willing to describe what happened to your family?"

Thorn frowned at that. "The details aren't important. It's enough to say that they were killed by *something* that spared me, likely by accident. Who knows? It marked me, but today I think its mind was more on feeding, and with three bodies to choose from, why pay close attention to a two-year-old?"

"When you found help, what did the law say?"

"Oh, the sheriff looked around. Measured some tracks, I think, although I couldn't swear to it. He finally concluded that it must have been a grizzly bear. No explanation for the season, why it wasn't hibernating when it should have been."

"You figure he was wrong." It didn't come out sounding like a question.

"At the time," Thorn said, "I didn't know. I had to grow into it, learn about the way bears live and feed, the cycles of their lives. I had to dredge up partial memories of what I'd seen, comparing them to pictures in my books. The first zoo that I ever saw opened in Providence, four years ago. They had a grizzly there. I stood outside its cage, staring, and couldn't make it jibe with what I saw before, or *thought* I'd seen."

"You were so young," Dinah replied. "And scared to death, I bet. It's only natural you'd be confused, so long after the fact."

"No doubt. It wasn't just confusion, though. I stood there, looking at that bear, and *knew* somehow it wasn't right. That won't make any sense to you, but I'm convinced it wasn't right. Whatever took my parents and my brother, it was...something else."

Instead of laughing at him, or commiserating, Dinah asked, "Like what?"

"If I knew that I'd have it solved, and maybe I could rest, instead of..."

"What?"

"The endless traveling, prying into dark corners where nobody else thinks I should go."

"Well, if it matters, I would disagree with that," she said.

"Being a newswoman."

"That's right. Nobody wants me nosing into *anything* that matters, anything that makes a difference. They'd like me writing stories about bake sales, flower gardens, and the latest style in women's clothes back east. Instead, I keep on digging, turning over rocks and making enemies."

"Sagrado's better for it, I imagine."

Dinah laughed at that and said, "After supper, you can read some of my hate mail."

"Sounds like some dessert."

"I hadn't planned dessert," she said. "I'm thinking steaks and baked potatoes, if that suits you. But dessert... How do you fancy something sweet?"

TWELVE

Dusk overtook them as they reached the outskirts of Sagrado, making Thorn glad that he hadn't tried to view another murder scene that afternoon. Tomorrow, he could get an early start and pick off two or three of the remaining farms, with any luck—not that he hoped for any startling revelations on the tour of broken hearts and dreams.

The hostler looked surprised when Thorn and Dina Pilcher brought their horses in together, but he asked no questions. Even so, he cut repeated glances toward them when he thought that neither one was watching him, trying to size the situation up and make sense of it for himself.

When they'd left the stable, Thorn said, "There's the next round of your gossip. He'll be telling people we were on a ride together."

"Well, we were," she said. "At least, the second half of it."

Thorn shrugged. "I have no reputation to preserve around Sagrado," he reminded her. "While you..."

"You're backing out of dinner, now?"

"No, Ma'am—I mean, Dinah."

"All right, then. Hold your head up, Gideon, and smile at anyone we pass along the way."

They passed six people before reaching Dinah's house, a bungalow with flowers set in window boxes and a bed of roses to the left of the front door as they approached. The small front yard was fenced with pickets painted white, and it contained an oak tree Thorn surmised was getting on toward twenty years of age. He waited on the porch while Dinah used her key, then followed her into a tidy parlor with a fireplace set into the northern wall.

"I like it," he told Dinah, when he'd had a look around. "I wasn't sure what to expect."

"You mean, no manly touches?"

"Well, I wouldn't go that far." He nodded toward a Henry rifle, standing upright in a corner close to the front door.

"It's not alone," she said. "I have a shotgun and six-shooter in the bedroom."

"For whoever sends the hate mail?"

"For whoever, period. A woman on her own, a town like this...Whether you're popular or not, it causes problems. Truth be told, it's possible to be *too* popular. People who thinks this girl's fair game are in for a surprise."

Thorn leaned his Winchester beside her rifle, at the door. He hadn't taken time to drop it off at the hotel, and was relieved now that it wouldn't be obtrusive in the room.

"Take off your gunbelt too, if you're inclined to," Dinah said.

He did, and left it curled up on a chair, saying, "We've got the makings of an arsenal."

She laughed and said, "I still hope no one tries to storm the fort."

"That could upset the appetite."

"Speaking of which, how do you like your steak?"

"I'm easy," Thorn replied. "Ideally, rare."

"Bloodthirsty," she observed.

"But only with my beef."

"And yet...no, never mind."

"Go on," he urged. "Say it."

"Well, in the kind of work you do, the cases you investigate, you must be used to blood and misery."

He thought about that for a moment, then replied, "It's too late for the victims who've been killed or injured by the time I reach a town, but I try not to dwell on that. If I examine wounds, it's with an eye toward finding out what caused them. Otherwise, I focus on preventing new victims from suffering."

"Please, Gideon, I didn't mean to say—"

"It's fine," he cut her off. "Your question's only natural. I ask myself some variation of the same thing, at least once a week."

"Thanks. And I'll try to keep the questions to a minimum, tonight. I'd love to find out more about your early life, though. I mean, from a tragedy in Colorado, and from there to Harvard, all that..."

"Money?" He was smiling when he added, "Don't forget the orphanage in Lawrence."

"Jesus! I stepped in it again!"

"Don't worry," he said, smiling. "It's all part of who I am today."

"And that," she said, "sounds like the biggest mystery of all."

"Not once you get to know me."

"Will I have that chance?"

"We've made a start, at least," Thorn said.

"And how's it going?" she asked, with a cautious smile.

"I was about to ask you the same thing."

"I'd say not bad. Not bad, at all."

Gabor faced Caprakan inside the farmhouse kitchen, seated facing him across the dining table as he questioned details of his lookout's story. "You are sure a woman traveled with him?"

"It was more as if she followed him, *hmen*. He seemed surprised to see her there."

"But they went in the house together, with the farmer's woman?"

"*He'le'*." Caprakan made sure to nod emphatically that he was sure.

"And stayed for some time, talking where you could not see them?"

Yaluk, watching from the sidelines, made a filthy joke about the three of them together, but his giggling died immediately when Gabor spun toward him, snarling at him like a rabid *ch'amak*. In the silence following, Caprakan said, "I suppose they must have talked, *He'le'*."

Gabor focused on him once again, asking, "And you are sure this second woman was the one from town, who prints the newspaper?"

"Yes, *He'le'*. I have seen her on the street, outside its office."

"Very well." The shaman sat in silence for a long moment, thinking, until Cadmael dared to ask him, "What can that mean, *He'le*?"

"Only one thing," Gabor said at last. "She and the

stranger are cooperating to defeat us. We must not allow it, when we are so close to victory for Kisin."

All around the table, voices echoed Kisin's holy name.

"But how can we prevent it, *He'le*?" asked Hunaphu, silent until then.

"By striking faster than they think is possible, and where they least expect it. We shall take the woman who dares meddle in our holy business, make her an example to the others, and leave only one task to fulfill."

All eyes turned toward Yatzil, the only woman in the room, who held her peace unless she was addressed directly by the shaman. Now, she simply smiled in recognition of her pivotal assignment in the drama moving toward its end. Her name in the old tongue meant "loved one," and each man inside the farmhouse could have said he truly loved her as a sister, although any thoughts that might have been lascivious were purged—at least in theory—from their minds and hearts.

Had anyone among them dared to touch her, Gabor's vengeance, aided by the others, would have been immediate and terrible.

"It is decided, then," Gabor told all of them together. "Make the necessary preparations. We shall leave within the hour to begin the final phase of reckoning."

"And if the man in black opposes us, *He'le*?" Ujarak asked.

"Eliminate him. Leave his body to confuse the townspeople while we proceed."

"So, how's your steak? Not too well-done?"

"It's perfect," Thorn replied, as soon as he had time to chew and swallow.

"Sorry," Dinah said. "I don't have that much company. Well, very little, when I think about it. Close to none."

Thorn understood her staying clear of any situation with the men in town that might spark gossip, but he asked, "Not even merchants' wives?"

"You'd be surprised," she said. "Some of them speak to me in passing, telling me they liked this editorial or that one in the *Sentinel*. But publicly, they line up with their husbands, rank and file."

"The men resent you most," Thorn said, not really asking.

"It's a status thing, in my opinion. Women have their place, but it's a man's world, and the preacher at the Free Will Church of God drives that point home whenever he can make it fit his sermon of the day."

"The Good Book," Thorn said, nodding. He had read it for a class at Harvard, on comparative religions, and he'd seen its many contradictions for himself, along with a presumed divine endorsement of such things as slavery, slaughter of children, and kidnapping "brides" in wartime, not to mention rape, if the attacker paid his victim's parents off and married her.

"That's it," Dinah replied, and quoted from the book of First Corinthians: " 'Let your women be silent in the churches, for it is not permitted unto them to speak.' Not in church, or anywhere else, if Reverend Jefferson had things his way."

"But you stand up to him, to all of them."

"For all the good it does," she said. "Sometimes, I think the smart thing would be just to pull up stakes and try a larger town, like San Diego. Did you know, they'll soon have twenty-seven *hundred* people there? That's half as many as Los Angeles, and growing by the day. Or, maybe San Francisco, with more people than the other two cities combined. I'm wasted in Sagrado, don't you think?"

"I'm not the one to ask," Thorn said. "You'd have to answer that one for yourself."

"I know. And isn't that pathetic, in itself? Why would I ask a man—a man I barely know—for his opinion on my life?"

Thorn shrugged and let that pass, waiting until he saw a chance to move the conversation back toward the ongoing murders that had brought him there.

"It's insecurity," she said. "That's what it is, and it's embarrassing. I make a decent living at my trade, despite the opposition of some old fogeys in town and all their wives who shy away from having an opinion as if it would give them warts."

Thorn couldn't help but laugh, then. "You've maintained your sense of humor, anyway."

"I need it," Dinah told him. "I can't let them catch me drinking."

Glancing toward her sideboard, he saw three bottles of wine and one of what he took to be cognac or some other liquor reserved for high society. "You still keep a supply on hand, though," he observed.

"But I have to be sly about it," Dinah said. "When a reporter from one of the larger dailies comes to visit, twice a year or so, I stock up, using them as an excuse."

"Adjust, adapt, and forge ahead."

"That might just be my epitaph."

"You're still a long way off from that," Thorn said.

"Don't be so sure. The average life expectancy of

women in the West is fifty-four years old. I'm over halfway there, for heaven's sake!"

"But bearing up quite nicely," Thorn replied. "I'd call you well preserved."

She nearly barked a laugh at that, then said, "Enough sweet talk! You'll turn my head."

A comfortable silence settled in between them, going on for several moments until Dinah said, "I guess we should talk more about the murders."

"I don't want to spoil your appetite," Thorn said.

"I'm made of sterner stuff than that."

"Okay. Do you have any theories on who might be doing it?"

"You weren't around to read my last couple of editorials," she said. "Taking away the victims' hearts intrigues me. That sounds callous, I expect, but—"

"No, go on. I know exactly what you mean."

"Well, I've looked into it. That kind of mutilation isn't new, you realize? Before the Spaniards ever landed in this hemisphere, heathens all over the Americas indulged in human sacrifices. Taking hearts was often part of it, as well as in the execution of their captured enemies. A brave man's heart, divided up among the warriors of a rival tribe, was thought to build their own courage."

"I thought the county sheriff and your marshal had ruled out attacks by Indians," Thorn said.

"Oh, *them*. Unless they find a body scalped and bristling with arrows, they discount the possibility of any aboriginal involvement." Seeing the expression on Thorn's face, she asked him, "What? I went to college too, you know. Not Harvard, granted, but—"

He raised a hand for peace. "Sorry. You took me by surprise, is all."

"My specialty," she said, and gave him back a crooked little smile.

"Like me, today, out at the Brokaw farm."

"I thought we might accomplish more, working together."

"So, you blame a tribe of Indians for what's been going on? Which one, if I may ask?"

"That's where I hit a snag," she said. "None of the local tribes, from the Cahuilla to the Manzanita and Jamul, have any history of human sacrifice. They've killed and mutilated enemies in battle, naturally, but nothing of this kind at all, that I can find in any reference."

"But you keep looking."

"Every day. Until somebody's brought to book for all of this, and citizens can rest in peace."

"Well, maybe there's a way to flush them out," Thorn said.

"Such as?"

"With bait, I guess. The fact is, I've been hoping someone would come after me. Sounds like a long shot, I suppose, but it's worked for me in the past."

"You must be confident in your abilities," she said.

"I'm still alive. At least, so far."

Dinah was frowning now. "And on that cheerful note," she said, "dessert?"

Dessert was apple pie with cheese, more talk, and finally—surprising Thorn no end—a soft kiss at the door before he stepped into the night. He was confused, wished he could stay, then caught himself scanning Sagrado Boulevard for watchers who might wish to turn the tender moment to their own advantage, using it somehow against himself or Dinah Pilcher.

Moving down the walk to her front gate, Thorn realized that nothing anybody said about their meeting could hurt him. He had no reputation to protect around Sagrado; no one in the town who mattered was expecting him to solve their problems or accomplish anything the sheriff's office or their marshal had not managed during weeks gone by. He was an interloper, butting in where almost no one wanted him to be.

Almost.

Dinah Pilcher seemed to want his help, and more, but was it fair of Thorn to linger only for the possibility of what might pass between them privately? That wouldn't crack the murder case, nor would it move Thorn any closer to an ultimate solution of his family's slaughter, more than twenty years ago.

And yet...

A mental voice was asking him what harm a little tenderness could do, between descents into the dark abyss of mystery. Part of him craved that closeness, even briefly, but another part immediately recognized the damage it could do to Dinah Pilcher, living in a small, judgmental town long after Thorn had ridden on to seek the next enigma, and another after that.

And so he didn't turn around, retrace his steps, knock softly on her door and ask if he could step inside once more. Whether the night had eyes on him or not—the marshal's nosy deputy or someone else in town—he wouldn't jeopardize her reputation and her livelihood for what amounted to a momentary fling.

Instead, he started toward the Easy Rest, dragging his feet reluctantly at first, then picking up his pace as he surrendered to resolve. Thorn was accustomed to a drifter's abstinence and knew it wouldn't kill him, even if it felt like hell right now. Tomorrow, maybe, he would see things in another light and—

When the crash of glass came, it was at his back and some distance behind Thorn. He could not have said with any certainty that it echoed from Dinah's house, but then he heard a woman's scream and recognized her voice as if he'd known it all his life.

Drawing his right-hand Peacemaker, Thorn turned and ran back toward the small house, with its picket fence and flowerbeds. He leapt over the fence at speed, advancing on the front door when he saw a lamp snuffed out behind the nearest windowpane, plunging the parlor into darkness.

Thorn was not about to stand on ceremony. He kicked in the door, followed his sweeping gun inside, and found himself immersed in chaos. Dinah screamed again, not close enough to reach her, but somewhere beyond a strangely shifting wall of hunched, distorted shadow-shapes that rustled when they moved. Thorn smelled something vaguely familiar, as if he had charged into a musty chicken coop, and then one of the shadow forms was rushing toward him, arms—or wings?—outspread as if it wanted to envelop him. He fanned two rapid shots into his adversary, point-blank range, and heard an almost human grunting sound as it dropped over backwards, sprawling with a dry rattle onto the floor.

No problem, then. If he could kill them—

Something had and solid slammed against Thorn's skull, behind one ear, before he had a chance to frame another target in his sights. Before the darkness took him down and out, he had time for one final thought.

His adversaries sounded, smelled, and looked like giant birds.

THIRTEEN

Thorn work to someone shaking him, shouting his name, unleashing waves of pain inside his skull. He fended off the clutching hands, opened his eyes to dim lamplight, and recognized the face of Marshal Pike not far above his own.

"All right, he's back," Pike told a group of men surrounding them. Their muttering subsided, as he asked Thorn, "Where is Dinah Pilcher? Can you tell us what happened, for God's sake?"

"Dinah?"

It was coming back to Thorn now, as he sat upright, regretting it at once, and probed his scalp with searching fingers. Blood had started clotting, covering a gash of sorts behind one ear, and while Thorn guessed his brain had taken quite a rattling, he found nothing to suggest a skull fracture.

Whoever knocked him out had not paused long enough to finish him.

Dinah.

Thorn struggled to his feet, assisted by the marshal, then fought waves of dizziness as he stooped to retrieve his hat and Peacemaker. The gun, he holstered, while he clutched the hat, unwilling to replace it on his head just know.

"Speak up, damn it!" the marshal snapped. "What happened here?"

"We had supper at her house," Thorn replied, "talking about the case. I started back to the hotel, then heard her scream. Glass breaking. Kicked my way inside and found—"

He paused to look around the parlor, crowded now by men he didn't recognize, as well as Pike's lone deputy. Some of the men were ranged around a figure laid out on the floor. Thorn pushed in that direction, feared the worst, then did a double-take as he discovered that the body wasn't Dinah Pilcher's, but apparently a man's.

He thought *apparently,* because the home invader was in costume, masked by a kind of helmet or headpiece that covered most of his face, concealing it behind colorful feathers and a curved, protruding simulation of a bird's beak. From the neck down, longer feathers cloaked the supine figure, hands protruding from the costume's fabricated wings, bare legs and feet extending from below the outfit's knee-length hem.

"A giant bird," Thorn muttered to himself, but loud enough for those surrounding him to hear.

"A man made up to look like one, at least," Pike said. "I guess we know what little Enzo meant. But where in hell is Dinah Pilcher now?"

"Taken away," Thorn said. "This birdman wasn't on his own. My guess would be I took them by surprise and they were worried that the gunshots would attract a crowd, so they left him behind and didn't finish me."

One of the men jamming the room stepped forward,

recognizable to Thorn at once as Reverend Jefferson. "Taken, you say?" the minister demanded. "Taken, where? For what ungodly purpose?"

"I can't answer that from what was left behind," Thorn said.

"But—"

"Never mind the guess-work," Marshal Pike cut in. "Let's try'n find out who this bastard is."

Bending over the corpse, Pike grabbed the costume's beak and gave a solid yank, revealing a Hispanic face and slicked-back hair.

"A goddamn Messican," the marshal's deputy spat out, then quickly added, "Sorry, Pastor."

Pinning Kuhn with gimlet eyes, the minister replied, "There's no excuse for taking the Almighty's name in vain."

"Forget that, now," Pike said. "I know this greaser."

"What? From where?" Thorn asked.

"He's one of 'em what works the former Albright farm, ten miles or so northwest of town. The Albrights, Joseph and his wife, packed up an left without a word to anybody, close to ten, eleven months ago. A couple months after they hit the road, this Mex callin' himself Jesús Cuevos showed up, wantin' to buy the spread. Me 'n Judge Engle checked 'im out, the best we could, but you know how them people are. No roots that anyone can trace to speak of, and he had the hard cash money, so..."

Thorn took advantage of the marshal's hesitation, asking, "And you say this man worked for him?"

"That's right. Called 'imself Emiliano Núñez, if I remember it aright."

"All right, then," Thorn replied. The former Albright farm it is."

"Hold on, now," Pike said, sounding vaguely sheepish.

"You should let the sawbones have a look at you. And anyway, the farm's outside my jurisdiction."

"So, you mean to let this pass?" Thorn challenged him.

"No, sir. I plan to contact Sheriff Coleman and—"

"Dinah could easily be dead by then," Thorn interrupted. He stopped short of adding *if she isn't dead already.*

"Well..."

Pike's deputy jumped in, saying, "I'm game if you are, Marshal."

"Charley, now—"

"I'm going, one way or another," Thorn announced. "I only need to fetch my my stallion from the livery."

Pike chewed on that a moment, then replied, "Okay, damn it. Charley and me'll come along and sort the law out later, if we make it back alive."

Pike grumbled all the way back to his office, warning Charley not to say another goddamned word if he knew what was good for him. Inside the office, Pike retrieved a Winchester from the gun rack, while Kuhn picked out a ten-gauge scattergun and started stuffing cartridges into his pockets till they bulged.

It seemed a long walk to the livery, folks watching them from both sides of Sagrado Boulevard, and when they got there, Thorn was mounted on his gray, the horse pacing around and anxious to be off. The hostler helped Pike saddle up his brindle gelding, then got Charley set up with his chestnut mare while Thorn waited outside, checking his watch to show he thought the pair of them were dragging ass.

When the two lawmen were mounted, they rode out to

meet the man in black and formed up flanking him, then started out of town at speed, veering to the northwest once they had cleared Sagrado's town limits.

Over the sound of hoofbeats, Thorn asked Pike, "How many other hands are working for this Cuevos, as you call him, on the Albright farm?"

"I'm sure of five," the marshal said, "but you kilt one of 'em in town. He's got a woman out there, too. Valeria, I think her name is. Took her for his wife, but never saw a ring on either one of 'em. Most Mexicans are Catholics, ya know, but that don't mean they ever made it to an altar, formal like."

"A woman," Thorn said, as if talking to himself. Then, back to Pike, "And all the other victims of these murders have been men?"

"Until tonight, yeah. It's the first time they snatched up a woman, and the first time they come into town."

"The pattern's changed," Thorn said.

"Pattern?" Charley chimed in. "What pattern, 'cept for cuttin' out the hearts?"

"Male victims," Thorn replied, "until tonight. The pattern may be changing."

"What in hell's *that* mean?"

Instead of answering the deputy, Thorn turned to Pike and said, "The feathers, Marshal."

"What about 'em?"

"Do you recognize them?"

"They were *feathers*. What are you—"

"I mean, the birds they came from? Did you recognize them that way, by their colors?"

"Nope. I never seen the like of 'em before."

"And from their size, I'd say they came from fairly large birds. Not as big as vultures or an eagle, but—"

"The hell are you ramblin' about?" asked Pike.

"The killers had to come from someplace where such birds are common," Thorn answered. "Are you familiar with the order Psittaciformes, Marshal?"

"Order what, to piss on who?"

"Parrots," Thorn defined it for him. "Brightly colored birds found in the tropics, all around the world."

"Parrots? You sayin' old Emiliano that you kilt in down had got dressed up in *parrot* feathers, with a phony beak to match? I can't tell if you're crazy, or he was."

"I wouldn't call him crazy, necessarily," said Thorn. "But *different,* oh yes."

"Would you start makin' sense, for Christ's sake?"

"Second that," the deputy put in.

Instead of answering directly, Thorn switched tracks again, asking, "What do you know about the rituals of human sacrifice?"

"A buncha heathen superstition," Pike shot back. "Ignorant savages killin' and eatin' one another, thinkin' it'll give 'em magic powers."

"Close enough," Thorn said, not quite disdainfully. "And do you know where rites like that were practiced, close to home?"

But Charley beat Pike to the punch on that one, calling out, "In Mexico?"

"That's right," Thorn said, "and father down, through most of South America. The Aztecs, Incas, Mayans, all had ceremonies that involved removing human hearts as part of their religious festivals."

Pike scoffed at that. "You're talkin three, four hunnerd years ago, at least, back when the Spanish come and turned 'em into Catholics."

"On paper, anyway," Thorn said. "But who's to say it stuck with everyone?"

Dinah Pilcher came awake to jolting, rhythmic motion, nearly smothered by a filthy-smelling rag someone had wrapped around her face and tied behind her head. It took a moment more for her to realize she was on horseback, but not seated upright as she was accustomed to. Instead, she had been draped across the horse's back, with someone else filling the saddle, guiding its progress. Despite the wrapping of her head, she heard more horses galloping to either side of her, guessing their number somewhere in the neighborhood of five or six.

The night's events came back to her in fractured images. She'd dined with Gideon, had dared to kiss him as he left, half-hoping he would overcome his principles and stay with her. When that fell through, she'd latched the door behind him, turned, and found herself confronting what she took for monsters in her sitting room—or, rather, humans dressed as monsters, garbed in feathers and grotesque headdresses, closing in upon her without saying anything.

She could remember fighting back and crying out, the sound of breaking glass—a lamp, perhaps; had they burned down her little house?—but then the home invaders overpowered her, clubbed her insensate, and apparently had bound her wrists and ankles prior to hauling her outside, placing her like a bedroll on one of the horses they had ridden into town.

The rest came back to her in fits and starts: feathers, the smell and feel of them as she was wrestled to the ground, then choked into unconsciousness; gunshots, together with a voice that might be Gideon's; the knowledge that she had been taken out of town, despite whoever tried to intervene, seeking to help. But *where* were her abductors taking her?

Dinah possessed a good sense of direction, but it failed entirely with her eyes blindfolded and blood rushing to her head, from her unusual position on the running horse. Aside from being certain they were long gone from Sagrado, well away from shouting townsmen and the prospect of pursuit, she could not guess the raiders' destination.

But she had a fair idea of why they wanted her.

Another murder in the offing, what else could it be?

Dinah had no idea why they would switch from killing eight men in a row to snatch their first female, or why it should be her. Was it her standing in Sagrado, as the town's newspaper publisher? That made no sense to her, but neither did kidnapping in the middle of the night.

She realized her focus now must be upon survival, if in fact she had a chance at all. Hands secured behind her, with her ankles likewise tied, she couldn't even fling herself from horseback to the ground, much less escape before the raiders reached wherever they were bound.

And on arrival there...

Dinah had seen some of the prior victims, with their chests slashed open and their hearts removed. Whatever motivated those atrocities, she couldn't help but see herself now, in her mind's eye, prostrate on the ground while she was being carved apart.

When they arrived, wherever they were going, she might have a small chance to resist, but with at least six men against her, maybe all of them deranged, she didn't like her odds. And yet, in spite of her extreme position, hopeless as it seemed, Dinah suppressed an urge to laugh out loud as one thought edged all others to the side.

She suddenly regretted that she wouldn't live to write and print the story of her own abduction by the murderers, allowing others in Sagrado a first-person glimpse inside the horror they'd been living with for weeks on end.

And there wasn't a damned thing Dinah could think of now, to save herself.

Thorn and his two companions stopped a quarter-mile before they reached the Albright ranch deciding it was best if they secured their horses where they stood and finished the approach on foot. Stealth raised the odds of them evading any lookouts posted on the spread, and taking those inside the lighted farmhouse by surprise.

Already whispering, as if afraid his voice might carry the 440 yards from where he stood to the old Albright place, Pike said, "Remember, now, we got no proof Miz Pilcher's in that house. The Mex Thorn shot was workin' here, but that don't mean the rest are in on what he done."

"No shootin', then, until we's sure?" his deputy inquired.

"No shooting, period, unless they start it first," Thorn interjected. "If they *do* have Dinah, they could use her as a shield or kill her just to spite us. Use your eyes first, count heads if you can, and be sure of what you're doing before anyone goes charging in."

"Supposin' we don't see Miz Pilcher," asked the deputy. "What, then?"

The marshal answered that one, saying, "If they's all

dressed up like birds, we go in strong. If not, we knock and tell 'em why we're there. See what they say."

"And then, it they try somethin'?" Charley Kuhn inquired.

"Defend yourself as necessary," Thorn chimed in, "while staying focused on our goal."

"Our goal?"

"Rescuing Dinah Pilcher," Pike growled at his underling.

"Oh, yeah."

They tied their horses loosely in a stand of cottonwoods and checked their weapons for the last time before setting out. Thorn had reloaded his Peacemaker after gunning down Emiliano Núñez, as the night-prowler was known in town, and now he made sure that his rifle had a live round resting underneath its hammer, ready for whatever happened next. He didn't relish killing, but it sometimes came with the life he had chosen, and Thorn had no regrets about the individuals he'd sent to their supposed reward. Each one of them along the way had been a murderer or worse. He lost no sleep over their deaths, and when he suffered nightmares, there were entities he feared much more than men with guns.

They made the first two hundred yards without a problem, watching out primarily for ruts or gopher holes that might twist ankles, or night-hunting rattlesnakes that might strike without warning if they were surprised. The waxing crescent moon cast pallid shadows out in front of them as they advanced, but so far, Thorn saw nothing in the way of human enemies or men disguised as animals.

Which didn't mean no lookouts had been posted, only that the would-be rescuers had not encountered them so far.

Thorn pictured Dinah Pilcher dead, slaughtered, and he felt a surge of nausea, quickly suppressed. He knew there had to be a method to the raiders' seeming madness. They could easily have murdered Dinah in her home, or in the dark outside, and it was easier to ride off with a heart than with a captive woman, maybe struggling, fighting for her life. The men who dressed like parrots *needed* her alive, at least up to a point. If they had brought her to the former Albright farm, there was at least a chance of finding her alive.

And failing that, then what?

Ideally, Thorn wanted to understand the killers' purpose and discover whether any others like them were at work, in other parts of California or the West at large. That meant capturing one of more of them alive, inducing prisoners to spill their darkest secrets, even knowing they were bound to hang for what they'd done.

Unlikely, Thorn supposed. But there was till justice to be imposed—or vengeance, in the grim alternative, for all the murderers had done so far. Thorn knew that Pike and Kuhn were fighting mad and scared to death, a combination of emotions that could easily unleash a massacre. And if it came to that, if killing were required to end the murder spree, Thorn knew which side he would be on.

The mystery remained unsolved, so far, but they were drawing closer to it, step by cautious step. A few more yards, and whatever came next lay resting in the hands of Fate.

FOURTEEN

Once inside what seemed to be a farmhouse, with her blindfold stripped away, seated in a straight-backed chair surrounded by her captors in their garish feather cloaks and helmets, Dinah Pilcher tried to put a brave face on her nearly paralyzing fear.

So far, her kidnappers had spoken only to each other, in a guttural, crude-sounding language she could not identify. Her first thought was that it must be some tribal dialect, which brought to mind the articles she'd read and written about women taken prisoner by Indians, the torture and the degradation they endured, assuming they survived at all. But something here was out of place. She knew that Indians might paint their faces and their chests for battle, wearing feathered headbands and all sorts of bones as necklaces, but the strange costumes ranged before her now seemed more like something from a fevered fantasy.

At last she found the nerve to speak, demanding of the group at large, "Why am I here? What's going on?"

One slightly taller than the rest, at least in his bizarre disguise, stepped forward, eyed her from behind his bright, beaked mask, and said in English, "You will help complete our summoning of Kisin."

Plain as mud.

Dinah frowned back at him and said, "Kitchen? What's that supposed to mean? What am I doing here?"

The seeming leader of the group strode forward, scowling from beneath his artificial beak, and struck Dinah across the face, an open-handed slap that rocked her on the wooden chair and left her ears ringing.

"The holy name is *Kisin*!" he corrected her. "Your foul mouth is unfit to speak it, so beware!"

Dina spat blood onto the floor in front of her and did her best to sneer at her assailant with red teeth and swelling lips. "It's not my fault that I don't speak your language," she replied, defiantly. "I want to know *right now* why you abducted me and what comes next."

The man who'd struck her took a backward step and hissed what might have been a low, derisive laugh. "You have a part to play in history, above your station as a mere white woman who knows nothing of the universe."

Again, as clear as mud.

"Can you explain it to me?" she demanded. "Or is that reserved for men in feathered capes?"

He paused, as if considering whether he ought to slap her face again, and then began instead to speak in stilted tones, almost like an instructor—or a preacher droning at a sleepy congregation from his Sunday pulpit.

"What do you know of history?" he asked.

"It was my major, back at Vassar. That's a college in—"

He raised a hand to silence her and asked, "You know the story of a land its natives call *Españia*?"

"Of course. That's Spain. In Europe."

"And you've read how, many years ago, they sailed to

our world and subdued it, as they thought? How they destroyed our people, cities, temples, and deceived themselves the old gods were no more?"

"Old Gods?"

"Kisin is the Lord of Death. Once in each thousand years, the stars align and we may call upon Him to relieve us of our enemies. The process calls for sacrifices, nine in all, to summon Kisin from the Underworld where He abides. When He returns..."

Dinah was busy counting in her head. So far, there had been seven murders on the farms around Sagrado, each man with his heart carved out. Is she was number eight...

"Hold on a second, will you? Please?"

The leader of her kidnappers regarded her with an expression of contempt, perhaps tinted by curiosity. "Your question?"

"You said nine killings—or sacrifices, as you say. There have been seven, up to now. All of the victims have been men."

A smile appeared below the sculpted beak. "And now you wonder what your role may be?"

She nodded silently.

"The last two sacrifices must be females, life-bringers. Their power rouses Kisin from below, and he consumes them avidly."

"So, I'm to be the eighth?" she asked.

The beaked head nodded silently.

"And who's the ninth, then?" Dinah queried him.

Instead of answering, the leader raised his long arms, draped in brightly-colored feathers, turned to face his followers, and said, "The circle shall be closed tonight! Glory to Kisin! Thank him for our sacred lands reclaimed!"

Thorn split off from Pike and Charley Kuhn when they had covered half the distance from their horses to the former Albright house. Both lawmen had seemed jumpy to him, likely second-guessing their decision since they'd left Sagrado, and he didn't want to be around them if they started arguing at the last minute, bringing guards down onto them with bickering or simple careless blundering on unfamiliar ground.

Two hundred yards and counting, but he'd still seen no lookouts in evidence around the house. That threw him off, thinking it seemed irrational. One of the killers lay dead, back in town, and Orrin Pike had recognized him instantly, as soon as he'd removed the dead man's strange helmet. Potter had named him as Emiliano Núñez, and he'd been accompanied by others in the raid on Dinah Pilcher's home. Those other guilty men had left him where he fell, which meant they had to guess he'd be identified, the Albright ranch a target of retaliation by the law.

What did it mean, if they had posted no lookouts around the spread?

Thorn's first thought was that Núñez, if that was indeed his name, had worked the Albright spread but done his killing with accomplices from elsewhere. Naturally, if the others hadn't carried Dinah Pilcher back to this farm, there would be no need for posted guards. In that case, Thorn assumed she would be dead by now, his rescue effort with the marshal and his deputy a total waste of time.

But that rang hollow somehow, in Thorn's mind. If the abductors simply wanted Dinah dead, her heart torn out, they could have killed her anytime and anyplace along the trail, once they had cleared Sagrado. Slicing out a heart was not a complex operation, not designed to heal, not when the victim was already marked for death.

Thorn's mind skipped tracks again. If Dinah *had* been brought back to the Albright farm, and not dumped heartless somewhere on the trail, then once again, why would a group of men acting with purpose post no guards? Were the kidnappers simply idiots? Not likely, if they had eluded capture in the first seven attacks. Were they deranged or blindly arrogant? Perhaps, but while their actions made no sense to Thorn, pure logic said the killings must make sense *to them*. There was a method to their seeming madness, which he'd not been able to detect as yet. Perhaps, if he caught one of them alive, for questioning...

Another reason struck him then: a notion that their purpose, still unknown to Thorn, had nearly run its course. The killers might be thinking they had time to finish off their grisly job—whatever *that* was—and that intervention by authorities would make no difference afterward.

That brought Thorn back to speculation on the workings of an unsound mind, and he cut off that line of speculation instantly. Each second he spent dwelling on unfathomable motives kept him from his goal of seeing Dinah Pilcher brought back to her home alive.

Despite his sense of urgency, Thorn slowed his pace over the last one hundred yards, knowing that any posted guards would probably be waiting there, where they were close enough to shout and warn others inside the house. He switched the rifle to his left hand, drew the twelve-inch Bowie with his right, prepared to strike without a sound if he encountered any living soul along the way.

But once again, he met no one.

Thorn closed in on the lighted house, working he way around toward the front door and windows he assumed must open on the largest of the rooms inside. Arriving there, Thorn sheathed his blade and cocked his Winchester, then set his hat beside him on the porch and leaned in close to peer inside. He knew that staring into darkness from a lighted room was hopeless, the reflection of lamplight blinding all those within to whatever was happening outside.

Eyes narrowing, Thorn saw five figures clad in feathered garb and beaked helmets, standing around a woman seated on a straight-backed wooden chair.

Gabor suspected he was wasting time, explaining his great mission to a captive, but in truth, he had been longing for an audience for months now, since the prophesy was first revealed to him and he was chosen by the gods to execute it. Wiping out the plague of whites was one thing, but he also wanted one of them, however small and insignificant, to understand *why* it was happening.

The prisoner had urged him on, asking, "What happens when these stars align?"

Behind his regal mask, Gabor could only smile at that. It was as if the woman were compiling notes for one of her newspaper articles—in this case, one he knew would never go to print. Why not indulge her curiosity a little longer, while he waited for the clock's hands to creep on around the dial toward midnight?

"When the stars are in their proper places," he replied, "Kisin draws power from the heavens. He emerges from his resting place below and walks the Earth once more, eliminating all our people's enemies with fire and lightning."

"When you say your people," she cut in, "who would those be, exactly?"

"Those usurped and driven out by white men long ago, their remnant left to wander in the wilderness, concealing their identity."

"Would I know them by any certain name?" she probed.

"We are the Yucatecs, or as your so-called scholars choose to call us in their dusty books, the Maya people."

That astounded her and left her gaping at him as he spoke again. "With Kisin's help, your filthy kind shall be eradicated from the lands that you have stolen over time, and from our Mother Earth throughout. Your day is coming to an end. Are you not proud to be the instrument of such a mighty change?"

Instead of answering his question, she tossed in another of her own. "And afterward, do your people repopulate the world? Where are they hiding? Do you even have enough to get it done?"

"With Kisin's help, all things are possible."

"I've heard our preachers claiming the same thing," she said. "Funny, it never seems to work for them."

"Because your creeds are false and have no power," Gabor said, with perfect confidence. Nothing the woman said to him could make him doubt his sacred mission now.

But still, she had more questions. "What do you imagine for the Earth, after your great apocalypse of fire and lightning?" she inquired. Her interest almost impressed Gabor as genuine. "Will anything be left?"

"The land shall be reborn," he answered confidently. "My people shall inhabit it as kings, serving the will of Kisin."

"Only kings?" she interjected. "What about the queens."

He frowned at that. "You are impertinent," he snapped.

"I tire of this. Prepare yourself for death with prayers to your selected deity, not that your cries will help you now."

Instead of quailing at his wrath, she seemed steadfast. "I only ask," she said, "because it's hard repopulating land with only men around."

At that, Gabor heard shifting sounds and whispered muttering among his followers. He glared them into quiet, then commanded, "Silence this blaspheming infidel! Prepare her for the sacrifice."

As if in answer to his sudden rage, there came a peal of thunder from outside, to eastward. At the same moment, a flash of lightning lit the sky beyond the farmhouse windows, turning the landscape deathly white, leaving its imprint on the shaman's retinas.

"You see, doubters?" he jeered at all of those assembled in the room. "The woman's words may sway you for an instant, but your god approaches in his wrath. Hail, Kisin! Welcome him with blood, and he shall free us from the plague that has oppressed our people for so long!"

The chant began then, as his feathered warriors moved to seize the captive woman, lift her from her chair, and turned to carry her outside. Their altar waited for her in the barn nearby, with candles ready to be lit. And after her, the final sacrifice, conducted on the stroke of midnight, would complete the ritual.

A new world lay within their grasp. Nothing could stop them now.

Thorn heard enough through the thin windowpane, each time the leader in his feathered costume spoke to Dinah Pilcher, that he understood at least a portion of the scheme behind Sagrado's recent homicides. It startled him, since history professors back at Harvard commonly described the Maya people as extinct—or nearly so—after the Spanish conquest of their native lands two centuries before, but he had evidence before his eyes that this small group of men, at least, were Mayans—or believed they were.

It made no difference to him, right here and now, if they were actual descendants of a nearly vanished race, or if they were insane and acting from a false conviction. He heard the leader of the small cult shout, "Hail, Kisin! Welcome him with blood, and he shall free us from the plague that has oppressed our people for so long!"

With that, the feathered followers closed in on Dinah Pilcher, reaching down to lift her from her chair. Cursing under his breath, Thorn wondered where the marshal and his deputy had gone, then eased back from the window, shouldering his rifle for a shot to stop the murder party in its tracks.

Before he squeezed the trigger, though, Thorn realized the costumed men did not intend to kill their captive on the spot, but rather to take her outside and away from the house. Thorn held his fire, deciding that a shot into the huddled group posed equal danger to the kidnappers and Dinah Pilcher. Once they cleared the house, perhaps his chances would improve—and his two missing sidekicks might appear to join the rescue effort after all.

Thorn backed off from the window, then stepped off the porch and crouched behind the nearest corner of the farmhouse. He was watching, rifle at the ready, when the cloaked kidnappers exited the building, several carrying their prey between them while she thrashed and struggled in their grip. None of them saw him watching from the pool of shadows there, in spite of lightning flashes that had started up short moments earlier, flooding the farmyard and surrounding structures with an eerie light. Behind each flash, a crack of thunder followed, even though the sky above seemed clear, speckled with stars.

So, what in hell was *that* about?

He shrugged it off, beyond caring about the strange weather when Dinah was in peril. As he watched, her captors bore her toward the barn, whose doors stood open on the night. While Thorn had been distracted by the scene inside the farmhouse parlor, someone seemingly had lit a lamp inside the barn, its pale light bleeding out into the darkness now, where only a black void was visible before.

Had he been spotted by whoever sparked the lantern? Thorn dismissed that thought at once, assuming anyone who'd seen him would have sounded an immediate alarm. Since no one had cried out, much less attacked him, he took it for granted that he'd passed unobserved. Likewise for Marshal Pike and Charley, his assistant, even though the pair of them was nowhere to be seen.

Thorn watched the feathered killers as they half-dragged and half-carried Dinah toward the barn. When they were safe inside, before they had a chance to carry out their foul design, he planned to rush the place alone, if necessary, and prevent their latest sacrifice at any cost. From what he'd heard while eavesdropping, Thorn took them for fanatics of the sort who won't surrender, even when their lives were on the line.

And that was fine with him.

He was prepared to kill them all, if necessary, if it helped get Dinah Pilcher home.

The shuffling, struggling group had reached the barn now, as another peal of thunder roared and lightning from a clear sky struck the ground, about one hundred yards away. Thorn left his hiding place and was about to make a mad dash toward the lamplight on the far side of the farmyard, when a hissing sound behind him froze him in his tracks.

He swung around, his rifle leveled, index finger on its trigger, and then held his fire as two familiar forms came toward him from the shadows. Marshal Pike was hissing at his deputy to shut him up, while Charley Kuhn muttered, protesting.

"All I asked you was—"

"For God's sake, Charley, shut your friggin' mouth!"

"Quiet, the both of you," Thorn snapped. "They're in the barn with Dinah now. We've got no time to waste. Come on!"

FIFTEEN

Dinah Pilcher struggled with her captors all the way between the farmhouse and the barn, cursing them bitterly in language that she rarely used, and wasn't even sure they understood. Despite her flailing, though, none of them struck her as they carried her across the open farmyard, as if honoring an order from their chieftain that they must inflict no further injury upon her until she was opened with a blade, her heart torn out.

And Dinah knew it wouldn't be much longer now.

After the darkness of the yard, she blinked against pale lamplight in the barn. Outside, thunder was rolling steadily, though she could not recall seeing a single cloud all day or after dusk. She'd missed the nearby lightning strikes while fighting for her life, but she had heard their crackling and her nostrils caught the scent of ozone on the night wind even now, inside the musty smelling barn.

When hostile hands released her suddenly, Dinah collapsed onto her knees, but then recovered, lurching to her feet, prepared to fight again. She had no realistic hope of breaking free, surrounded as she was, but in her desperation she determined that her captors would not celebrate her death without fresh scars to show for it. If flesh wounds made them recognizable around Sagrado, she might even be responsible in part for bringing them to justice, somewhere down the line.

But Christ, she didn't want to die!

Before her feathered escorts closed on her again, Dinah made out the shape of a long, sturdy table they had set up in the barn, midway between the open front doors and a smaller exit at the rear. She recognized it as an altar, with its decorations made of bones and feathers dangling from rawhide thongs, but saw no bloodstains on the wooden planking yet. Surprised at first, she quickly understood the reason for its cleanliness. So far, the other sacrifices had been carried out where victims lived, without transporting them intact to the old Albright farm. And it made perfect sense—at least, as much as anything else Dinah had endured on this long night.

Her sacrifice was *special.* They had brought her here to take their time, perhaps increase her torment, and to carry out a more elaborate performance for their so-called "god," Kisin.

But she was not to be the final victim, if the leader of her captors had been speaking truthfully. And with that fact in mind, she had to ask herself: *who's next?*

Would it be someone Dinah knew, someone else snatched from town? That seemed illogical, since she knew her abduction would have raised a hue and cry. Whether it prompted Marshal Pike to leave his narrow jurisdiction and come after her was anybody's guess, another waste of time for worrying, when she appeared to have so little left.

And Gideon? Dinah had heard gunshots as she was carried off into the night, but didn't know who'd fired them. Had he heard her stifled scream and doubled back in an attempt to help her? Had the raiders killed or wounded him before they fled with her into the night?

Dinah marshaled her strength and swallowed down the bitter taste of fear, facing the costumed men who meant to kill and mutilate her within moments now. She crouched slightly, the better to lash out at them with kicks and fingers curled like claws when they took hold of her. She wished for longer fingernails, to rend them with, but Dinah kept them short for working on her Remington typewriter, and to keep from breaking them when she set type for new editions of the *Sentinel.*

So be it. She would fight with what she had.

The leader of the freakish cult had moved to stand beside their makeshift altar, drawing a long dagger with a curving blade from somewhere underneath his feathered robe. Arms spread as if preparing to be crucified himself, he cried out to the barn's high, vaulted roof, "Lord Kisin! Hear my plea and join us now! Your final offerings await you!"

Dinah had steeled herself to curse and laugh at that, but she was silenced by another crack of thunder that sent shudders through the barn, dust sifting down around them from its hand-hewn beams.

"You go around in back," Thorn ordered Pike and Kuhn, without regard to their authority as lawmen. "I'm taking the front. You hear me shooting, come on in and do the best you can. Remember Dinah's in there. Only shoot the kidnappers."

"Shouldn't be hard," Pike said, "all feathered up the way they are."

"The hell is that about?" Kuhn asked.

"Forget it," Thorn commanded. "We can talk about that later." Almost adding, *If we're still alive.*

He watched the mismatched officers sprint off and vanish into darkness on the east side of the barn, then Thorn closed on the open double doors where lamplight streamed into the thunderous night. Another bolt of lightning strobed across the sky, off to his left, bathing the farmyard in its pale light for perhaps a second and a half.

And from inside, he heard a deep voice calling out, "Lord Kisin! Hear my plea and join us now! Your final offerings await you!"

Some kind of a religious ritual, although Thorn didn't recognize the name pronounced. His studies of the mainstream and occult religions, carried out at Harvard and at home, under the tutelage of Aunt Drusilla and her Spiritualist friends, had not included any deity named Kisin that he could recall.

No matter. Thorn was not required to recognize their god by name, much less believe in him or it, to realize his adversaries were committed to the strange rites they had carried out so far, and were about to replicate with Dinah Pilcher as their latest victim. As he neared the barn transformed into some kind of pagan temple for the night, he hoped that Marshal Pike and Charley Kuhn had found their proper place around in back.

Because he was prepared to interrupt the ritual of death as best he could, with or without their help.

Another lightning strike came out of nowhere, shattering an outbuilding Thorn took to be the former Albright privy, fifty yards or less away from him. The air crackled with static, and he felt the short hairs rising on his nape, stirring along his forearms even underneath his shirt and jacket sleeves. His ears rang from the lightning's impact, but Thorn still heard chanting from within the barn.

Thorn glanced away just long enough to see the blasted outhouse, now in smoking ruins. Farther out, where flat gray land met inky velvet sky, his eyes picked out a seeming whirlwind forming to the east, its outline ghostly pale as it began to writhe and undulate across the plain.

A second's observation told Thorn it was headed for the Albright farm.

Now, what in hell is this?

He had no time to ponder it, or wonder what would happen if the growing cyclone swept across the farmyard. Thorn was focused on his mission now, to the exclusion of all else. The freakish weather simply had to wait its turn.

Grim-faced, he clutched his Winchester and stepped into the light.

"What 'n hell is goin' on out here?" asked Charley Kuhn, his hoarse stage whisper covered by another peal of thunder.

"Never mind that now," hissed Marshal Pike. "We got a job to do."

"But Orrin, shit! This weather—"

"Will you shut the hell up, now!" Pike challenged, brandishing his Winchester as if he meant to smack Kuhn with its hardwood stock. Kuhn's mouth snapped shut and Pike turned from him, jogging on around the barn to reach the access door in back.

He wondered whether they were already too late for Dinah Pilcher, thinking maybe when the shooting started and they took Thorn's lead, busting inside, they might not find her dead and gutted like the other victims in the murder string so far. That would be grim, by God, but there would be a kind of consolation in it, anyway, killing the men responsible, with no one capable of second-guessing whether he and Charley could've brought them in alive.

With seven murders—maybe eight, now—Pike was in a killing mood himself, not giving any thought to what might happen afterward. He faced a reelection bid next year, if he decided it was worth keeping the job, and taking out the crazy killers with his own hand wouldn't do Pike any harm with voters in Sagrado, even though some might still hold a grudge against him for the wasted time before he got it done. The good news was that he could blame the bulk of that on Sheriff Coleman and his people, doing piss-all at the county seat, and it would likely stick. He'd lose a sort of friend that way, but keep his job—again, if that was what he cared to do.

Rounding the final corner, just a few steps from the barn's backdoor, Pike thought that playing lawman might have run its course. The truth be told, his zeal had been declining, right along with his performance for a period of years, moving Pike on from large towns into smaller ones, until he finally wound up guarding a wide spot in the road.

But if he left the law behind, what else would he be suited for? He was too old for punching cows, lacked the experience to drive a herd himself, and when he thought of settling down and raising crops, his stomach twisted into sour knots.

Pike didn't realize that he had stopped until his deputy ran into him and nearly made him drop his Winchester. The marshal whipped around, snarling, and saw Charley retreat a couple steps, eyes wide with fright.

"S-s-sorry," Kuhn stammered, clutching the ten-gauge to his chest.

"Just watch it!" Pike instructed, then turned back and started creeping toward the barn's rear door.

It wasn't standing open, but the latest tenants hadn't latched it from the inside, either. Dropping to a half-crouch, Pike began to ease it open, one inch at a time, praying the hinges wouldn't squeal and give their game away. They didn't, for whatever reason, and he took a hasty peek inside the barn, saw roughly half a dozen men dressed up in crazy feathered garb just like Emiliano Núñez had been when he died, then lost count of them when he spotted Dinah Pilcher in their midst. One of the costumed men was leading, while the others hustled her along toward a crude wooden table standing in the center of the barn.

Pike mouthed a silent curse. He didn't have to guess what they were planning when they got her laid out on the table like a side of beef ready for butchering. He shot a quick glance back at Charley Kuhn and found his deputy staring straight at him with a vaguely stunned expression on his face, ready to move on Pike's command.

At least he hadn't run away, though Pike could see him trembling while the thunder rolled—and there was something else now. What, exactly? Straining with his ears, Pike made it out to be a sound of rushing, swirling wind.

Terrific. A tornado's all we need right now.

"We goin' in, or what?" Kuhn asked, voice barely audible.

Pike shook his head and answered back, "We wait for Thorn to start the ball, just like he said."

"What if they picked him off?" Kuhn hissed.

"We got a minute, yet," Pike said. And turned his full attention back to the bizarre procession in the barn.

Gabor, the shaman, gloried in the night sounds from outside the lamplit barn. They told him that Lord Kisin was preparing to accept his final sacrifices and appear to bless them for their efforts at the stroke of midnight on this holiest of nights. He did not need to check the watch he carried underneath his feathered robe. It was enough to hear the thunder and the rising wind, shot through with lightning bolts delivered with a rising tempo, like no storm Sagrado and environs had experienced before, or ever would again.

Their world was on the cusp of changing, where the white plague would be swept away by fire, and the ancestral lands of his proud people finally restored, nearly four centuries after the first invaders brought their flags and armored troops ashore to plunder all before them in the name of their impotent god.

Gabor had wondered, in his childhood, why Lord Kisin did not simply rise to strike down the invaders then, sink their pathetic sailing fleets and move on back to Europe, leveling their cities and their castles, wiping out their kings. Only as an adult, schooled as the final shaman of his race, was he instructed that Lord Kisin was, Himself, a subject of the heavens, bound to rise and fall according to the stars. Throughout his life, Gabor had waited patiently for the alignment he required to bring about the epic change, and now that it had come, he would not miss the only chance provided for another thousand years.

Behind him, he could hear the captive woman struggling, cursing at the escorts who conveyed her to the waiting altar. Every note of rising terror in her voice was music to the shaman's ears. Lord Kisin feasted on the fear and pain of sacrificial offerings—until the final, willing acolyte whose life was offered voluntarily, an avid gift of pure devotion.

"*Beora!*" Gabor snapped at his disciples, urging them to greater haste. The final sacrifice accomplished by brute force should be completed within moments, then the last one could begin, concluded on the very stroke of midnight when the stars and planets were aligned. Lord Kisin waited, and Gabor would not allow his triumphant return to be aborted by a clutch of sluggish worshipers.

The altar stood before him now, and Gabor moved aside, drawing his dagger as he cleared a path for the delivery of their eighth victim to her death. Once she was splayed out on the planking, it would be the work of only seconds to rip through her clothing and her tender flesh, to reach inside and lift her warm, still-beating heart on high.

Above them, as his men lifted her writhing body, lightning struck a weather vane mounted atop the barn. Its impact rattled walls and beams, showering Gabor and his feathered acolytes with dust accumulated over years. The shaman looked up, half expecting flames to be enveloping the barn's roof now, but he saw nothing of the kind.

Of course. Lord Kisin held the key to weather and all nature in his mighty hands. He would not let his summoning be interrupted now.

Gabor's men raised their captive off her feet and laid her face-up on the altar. Even now she struggled, but the four of them restrained her arms and legs with no apparent difficulty, staying out of reach when she snapped at them like a cornered animal. Her will to live was powerful indeed, and all that energy would be transmitted to Lord Kisin when Gabor retrieved her heart.

Beneath his feathered robe, Gabor imagined he could feel his gold watch ticking, urging him to strike without further delay. Smiling beneath the curved beak of his helmet, he began the chant that would release her spirit to the night and its divine recipient. His acolytes joined in at once, their voices merging into one as they pronounced the sacred words.

Gabor moved closer, thighs pressing against the altar's rough-hewn planks, and raised his gleaming dagger overhead.

Gideon Thorn watched over rifle sights as the disguised kidnappers lifted Dinah Pilcher off her feet and placed her on the table they'd erected in the barn. He hadn't risked a shot while they were dragging her past empty stalls and bales of moldy hay, but now the leader of the group had stepped into position, blocking out Thorn's view of Dinah as he raised a long knife and prepared to strike.

The shot would be a gamble, but he had to try it, aiming high enough to miss Dinah completely on the makeshift altar, while preventing her intended murderer from striking, or at least distracting him. The upraised, feathered arm made an inviting target, crimson in the ambient lamplight, but Thorn worried that he might miss his mark and give the madman time to strike with lethal force, unless—

He had no further time to think about it now. The fist and knife had reached their apogee, preparing to descend, when Thorn released his pent-up breath and squeezed the rifle's trigger. Two hundred grains of lead left the Winchester's muzzle, closing the forty-foot gap in less than one-third of a second, striking his target with 688 foot-pounds of energy. A puff of blood and feathers filled the air down range, and Dinah's would-be murderer pitched forward, sprawled across her supine form. The other costumed men all spun around to gape at Thorn, resembling a clutch of startled parrots interrupted at a meal.

Those feathered men were moving now, preparing to attack Thorn and disarm him if they could—or die in the attempt—when more gunfire erupted from behind them, coming through the barn's backdoor. A rifle shot rang out, and then a heavy shotgun blast reverberated through the barn, dropping one of the plumed fanatics in a cloud of feathers, red, yellow and orange.

A shout went up from the remaining cultists, voiced in some language Thorn didn't understand. Of those still on their feet, two faced toward him, while a third was staring toward the backdoor, where now Marshal Pike and Charley Kuhn were barging in to join the party. Thorn had eyes on Dinah Pilcher, pinned beneath the man he'd shot at first, trying to see if she'd been wounded by the shotgun blast a moment earlier. Before he had a chance to tell, the group's leader lurched upright once again, grabbed Dinah by her hair, and pressed the curved blade of his dagger to her straining throat.

Thorn sighted past the other kidnappers, trying to draw a bead on Dinah's captor that would not unduly put her life at risk, and in the meantime, Pike and Kuhn were busy taking down the others. Pike dropped one more with his Winchester, then Kuhn unleashed the second barrel of his scattergun, peppering two more with leaden buckshot pellets. Both were wounded, but that didn't stop them—barely slowed them down, in fact—as they came galloping toward Thorn on what he saw were bare feet, howling incoherently and flapping feathered arms as if they planned on taking flight.

Only as they approached him did Thorn realize that

both men had drawn daggers of their own. Neither was curved or as ornate as what the leader held to Dinah's throat, but both looked long and sharp enough to do the job, if either one of them got close enough to make a killing lunge.

Cursing bitterly, Thorn tore his eyes away from Dinah Pilcher and the man who held her as a human shield, shifting his rifle and his full attention toward the underlings intent on killing him. Beyond them, he could just see Pike and Kuhn standing inside the barn, both with their weapons trained on Dinah and the madman holding her.

Thorn cried out to them. "No! Don't shoot!" before his own attackers closed the gap and he was forced to put the woman out of mind, trying to save his own life first, before he could save hers.

SIXTEEN

The two runners had nearly closed on Thorn before he shot one in the face and blew away the curved beak on his helmet, baring what remained of an imploding, bloody face beneath. The dead man staggered on another step or two, glancing off Thorn's left shoulder as he fell and causing Thorn to lurch backward in turn.

There was not time to pump his rifle's lever-action then, much less to draw one of his Peacemakers, before the second enemy let out a howl of rage and fell upon him, dagger slashing downward toward Thorn's face. Thorn blocked it with his rifle, saw a spark fly from the Winchester's receiver as the blade made ringing contact, then he lashed hack with the rifle's stock, clubbing his adversary squarely in his feathered chest.

The costume's padding took most of the blow, but Thorn was strong enough to force the shrieking cultist back a step or two. Next time the madman launched himself with knife outstretched, Thorn swung his long gun yet again, a spent round still inside its chamber, coming up beneath the killer's chin to stun him as his head snapped back, beak pointed toward the barn's high raftered ceiling.

That was all Thorn needed for a backward step, swinging the rifle clear in his left hand, clutching its barrel, while he drew the Colt from his right hip, cocked it, and pumped a round into his adversary's feathered chest. Whatever else the costume did for members of the rabid sect, it wasn't bulletproof. Blood spouted from between the rows of overlapping feathers, and his man went down, his final cry of rage transformed into a gargling as he died.

That left the leader of the pack, still using Dinah Pilcher as a shield while facing down Sagrado's marshal and his deputy. Both lawmen had their weapons leveled at their last surviving enemy, but neither dared to fire, for fear of drilling Dinah if they did. Sensing their hesitation, knife still pressing Dinah's throat so tightly that it loosed a tiny stream of blood, the madman snarled at them in English, with an accent that reminded Thorn of southern Mexico.

"Put down your weapons!" he commanded. "You shall not prevent the sacrifice!"

"Too late," Thorn said, as he approached the grim tableau. Recalling what he'd heard while eavesdropping, he said, "You had to finish up by midnight, yes? With all this ruckus going on, looks like you missed your chance."

It was a gamble, desperate at that, since Thorn had no real idea of the time. For all he knew, the stroke of midnight might have fallen, or he could have missed it by five minutes, either way. Still, it was all he had to stay the killer's hand and buy Dinah more precious time.

"You lie!" the shaman spat at him. "The planets are aligning, even now!"

"You think so?" Thorn replied, a challenge in his tone.

"Why don't we go outside and see. You'd have no trouble telling from the stars, right?"

"I am not so easily deceived, white man!" And saying that, the killer raised his knife just far enough to thrust it downward, into Dinah Pilcher's throat.

There are moments in a frontierswoman's life, whether she's "citified" or not, when instant action is required to halt—or, at the very least, to minimize—disaster in the making. Dinah Pilcher didn't have to guess what was about to happen when the lone survivor of her kidnappers, facing three armed men prepared to cut him down, reared back and raised the dagger he'd been holding to her throat a heartbeat earlier.

Gideon Thorn had tried to talk the madman into thinking that his superstitious deadline had elapsed, that killing her beyond midnight would be a waste of time, but his best effort was in vain. Another second, maybe less, and Dinah knew the dagger's blade would plunge full-length into her throat, perhaps her chest, and that would be the end of her. Thorn and his companions would immediately kill the man responsible, but it would be too late for her, blood pumping from her final wound in quantities no human hand could stanch.

So it was down to Dinah, and she had to make her move *right now.*

Instinctively, she kicked back with her right boot, mindful that her would-be murderer was barefoot. Putting all the force she had behind it, her boot heel raked his naked shin beneath the feathered hem of his disguise, and Dinah threw her full weight back into a crushing blow atop his instep. She felt small bones crack and heard her captor wail in pain, recoiling from her just enough for Dinah to crouch down a bit, twist in his grasp, and drive an elbow hard into his groin.

The madman's wail became a bellow, rage mingled with pain, while Dinah slid out of his fumbling grip, dropping to hands and knees before him. Outside, another clap of thunder rocked the barn, then it was suddenly eclipsed by three guns going off at once. Their muzzle flashes seared her eyes as Dinah dropped further and flattened to the barn's floor, conscious of deadly projectiles passing overhead. She cringed at wet, raw smacking sounds as rifle bullets and a storm of shotgun pellets found their mark, willing herself to swallow back a cry of fear.

That second seemed to stretch interminably, going on forever in her mind. Still fearful that the lunatic might topple forward, slashing at her as he fell, she braced herself for anything. A moment later, as she cringed, Dinah could feel feathers alighting softly on her back and shoulders, followed by a drizzling crimson mist of blood.

Thorn fired one round into the howling cultist's chest, then watched as Marshal Pike and Charley Kuhn finished him off with Winchester and shotgun fire. The impact of their nearly point-blank rounds lifted the killer off his feet and blew him backward, soaring almost like the bird he chose to emulate, arms spread and mutilated feathers trailing in his wake. Before he hit the barn's floor, dead beyond the shadow of a doubt, Thorn was already kneeling next to Dinah, reassuring her with gentle words, helping her rise to stand upright on trembling legs.

"I reckon that's the end of it," said Kuhn, to no one in particular.

Outside, there was no lessening of thunder, lightning, or the rumbling of ferocious wind. Thorn wondered whether they should fall back to the farmhouse, taking shelter from the storm until it passed before returning to Sagrado, but he never got the chance to ask Dinah or either of the lawmen who were busily reloading firearms.

From the shadows ranged behind Pike and his deputy, where hay bales had been stacked by Joseph Albright, then abandoned when he and his wife had left their farm, a shrill screech echoed through the barn. Thorn turned in that direction, startled, and was just in time to see an apparition leap from hiding, rushing toward their little group.

He saw it was a woman, dark-skinned and bare-chested, long hair streaming out behind her, decorated like a feathered headdress, with her face distorted in a snarl. He couldn't understand what she was screaming, though the name "Kisin" stood out, and at the moment, any words she spoke were immaterial.

The late arrival's right hand clutched a long knife rather like the former shaman's dagger, slashing with it as she reached the two lawmen. Their stunned reaction time was slow, their faces gaping at their new, half-naked, wholly unexpected enemy.

Before Thorn could react, the woman whipped her knife across the marshal's throat, unleashing blood that geysered from the open wound, splashing her face as much as it covered his own. Pike gasped a gargling sound, collapsing backward as the woman turned and struck again, this time aiming at Charley Kuhn. She missed his throat but plowed a gash across his left cheek, just below his eye, and dropped the sobbing deputy to hands and knees.

Thorn was retreating, trying to support Dinah with one hand, raise his rifle with the other, realizing that he hadn't pumped its lever-action after firing on the shaman seconds earlier. Stymied, he tried to block the knife thrust being aimed at him, but he reckoned without the screaming woman's speed, her animal agility.

Thorn felt the blade strike, ripping through his shirt and flesh, then glancing off a rib. He staggered backward, lost his grip on Dinah's arm, and falling, saw the woman they'd all overlooked reclaim the shaman's hostage, fingers tangling in Dinah's hair and dragging her away from Thorn, off toward the barn's wide-open double doors.

Thorn struggled to his feet, leaving his Winchester where he had dropped it, left hand clutching at his wound, drawing a pistol with his right. He spared a backward glance toward Pike and Kuhn—the former clearly dead or dying, while the deputy was out of action, hands clasped to his bloodied face—then trailed behind the two women already disappearing through the barn's doors, out into the storm-lashed night.

Yatzil—"loved one" to other members of her sect, now lying dead—had waited, hiding in the shadows, for the scene before her to play out. She hoped Gabor and her surviving brothers would destroy the three white interlopers and proceed with the appointed sacrifice that night, which she would follow as the ninth and only voluntary offering to Lord Kisin. The final touch was necessary for His summoning, but now, with Gabor and the rest shot down by infidels, she'd known that it was her time to appear and make things right, before their dwindling time ran out.

It had been easy for her, taking down the two lawmen before they even knew that she existed, slashing and disabling them before they turned their guns her way. The third man—first to spring upon her shaman and her brothers in the barn—was quicker than the two townsmen, but Yatzil had stabbed him, as well. Not mortally, perhaps, but deep enough to slow him down and let her do what must be done.

The white woman struggled against Yatzil, but she was weakening and lacked the Mayan girl's raw strength, much less her dedication toward completion of Lord Kisin's holy ritual. As Yatzil dragged her captive from the barn, she glanced off to the north and saw the out-of-season cyclone spinning rapidly, collecting dust and small stones from the earth below, but not advancing further toward the farm.

Lord Kisin waited for his final offerings, one wrenched by force from a white infidel, the other given up with gratitude and love.

Yatzil had not planned for this moment, just this way. Of course, why would she? If the white men had not interfered, she would have watched Gabor dispatch the woman from Sagrado's newspaper, then Yatzil would have moved to take her place of honor on the altar, singing words of praise to Lord Kisin before the knife fell one last time, cleaving her chest open and offering her warm, still-beating heart to Him.

Nine sacrifices, timed precisely, with a few moments remaining until midnight on this Night of Nights. Yatzil's idea might not fulfill the plan precisely, but she *could* offer Lord Kisin his two hearts, if only He supplied her with sufficient strength.

And once she'd plied the dagger's blade against her own flesh, He could reach down from on high and claim her heart Himself. What better climax to the ritual Yatzil had been imagining and looking forward to all year?

Dragging the white woman behind her, Yatzil raised her voice to rumbling, flashing heaven, eyes locked on the swirling cyclone as, within it, her Lord Kisin started to assume a shape more recognizable to Yatzil's eyes. With any luck, she'd be allowed to look upon him, see him fully in the final seconds of her life on Earth, before he whisked her off to glory in the stars.

Another moment now, and she would be released, a heroine enshrined in history for total dedication to her God.

Gideon Thorn lurched through the barn's wide-open door, fighting a ruthless wind that tried to push him back inside as if it were a sentient thing, allied with his female opponent toward the goal of Dinah Pilcher's death. Grit stung his face and made him squint before the howling wind whipped off his hat and flung it back inside, making a hopeless tangle of his hair.

Despite that wind, the flying dirt and sand, Thorn had a relatively clear view of the farmyard, spotted Dinah Pilcher in her would-be slayer's grip as they proceeded toward the towering cyclone, less than one hundred feet before them now.

The cyclone... What on Earth?

Thorn tore his eyes away from Dinah and her captor, staring at the whirlwind now. He could gave sworn that it was more than simply thrashing, spinning wind whipped up by the bizarre nocturnal thunderstorm and lightning. There appeared to be something *inside* it, filling up the cyclone with its height and girth, a not quite human form, yet human*like,* possessed of head, torso and limbs, all in their roughly normal places, on a giant scale.

Thorn reckoned he must be hallucinating, keyed up by the human sacrifice they'd almost managed to prevent, shocked by his knife wound and resultant loss of blood—but why, then, could he see the looming figure in the cyclone *moving* as if powered by its own volition, long legs taking one step forward, then another, stout arms rising, reaching out toward Dinah Pilcher and the female cultist bent on killing her?

Ignore it, he thought, focusing on what he had to do, and quickly now, before it was too late.

Thorn drew one of his Colts, cocked it, and took the free hand from his open wound to steady his gun hand. He'd have one shot, at most, before the woman's dagger finished Dinah where she stood—and if his arm was shaking, if he missed, his bullet might strike Dinah down before the madwoman could manage it herself.

He aimed, his eyelids narrowed down to slits against the rising wind, half-blinded by the nonstop lightning flashes, ears numbed by the thunderclaps that came in rapid fire, like field artillery. Finding his target in the windswept night, Thorn held it, squeezed the trigger of his Peacemaker, felt it recoil against his palm and saw its muzzle flash, although the echo of that shot was snatched and whipped away, skyward.

Down range, he saw the nearly naked woman with the dagger arch her back, half-turning toward him with a snarl of pure animal fury on her face. She lost her grip on Dinah Pilcher at the same time, wailing as her captive ducked and rolled away, beyond her reach.

In front of her, it seemed to Thorn that he could see the giant from the cyclone striding forward, fanged mouth open wide and howling loud enough to make the thunder fade away. Long arms with broad, six-fingered hands, the fingers tipped by talons, reached down for the half-dressed woman, closed around her, lifting her, then gave a brutal twist that ripped her thrashing form in two around the waist, tossing her high and wide like so much wind-blown trash. A crimson storm of offal fell, splattering Dinah where she lay cringing, her face pressed to the soil.

Thorn tried to cock his Peacemaker again but felt it slipping from his grasp. A second later, he sprawled facedown in the yard and darkness swallowed him alive.

SEVENTEEN

JUNE 8, 1876: SAGRADO

Doctor Reuben Baldridge cleaned Thorn's wound and closed it with six stitches, telling Thorn he had been lucky that his enemy was rushing and distracted when she'd stuck him. She'd done worse to Marshal Pike, throat slashed and dead from loss of blood before he could be helped, and Charley Kuhn had forty stitches in his ravaged face, still unable to speak coherently.

Small favors, Thorn decided, as he left the doctor's office and nearly jostled Dinah Pilcher where she stood, outside.

"How are you, Gideon?" she asked, clutching his sleeve and drawing him aside. There would be no escaping prying eyes today, much less interrogation by the county sheriff, if and when he made the trip to town.

"Better than some," Thorn answered, letting Dinah lead him more or less in the direction of her office at the *Sentinel.*

"I know," she said. "Orrin and Charley Kuhn. I owe the three of you my life."

"You did all right yourself, as I recall."

She tried to force a smile at that, but barely managed it. Voice hushed, eyes darting up and down the sidewalk, she told Thorn, "I didn't tell the doctor about anything we saw. Did you?"

Thorn shook his head. "I doubt that he'd believe it, anyway."

"And Sheriff Coleman? I mean, when he gets here, will you...?"

"Doubtful," Thorn replied. "From what I've heard about him, he likes simple answers, and I wouldn't want a one-way ticket to the lunatic asylum."

"So, what *will* you tell him? What should *I* say?"

"My advice is keep it basic. There've been murders in the area. He knows that much already. The killers snatched you, but you don't know why. I shot one of them here in town, and went to find you with the marshal and his deputy. The rest of it is pretty much straightforward, all the shooting, stabbing, people dying. He can go out to the farm and see it for himself, whatever's left after the storm."

"And what about that storm?" There was a tremor in her voice this time. "We both saw..."

"Something," Thorn agreed. "But what? How would you put it into words the sheriff will believe?"

"That's what I'm trying to decide."

"All right. Here's what we know. After the fight inside the barn, a woman came from hiding, killed the marshal, slashed his deputy and me, then dragged you out into the yard, to finish what the others started. It was storming. I already talked to Doctor Baldridge, and he heard the thunder, saw the lightning. So did anybody else in town who wasn't fast asleep."

"They didn't see what happened at the farm," Dinah reminded him.

"Correct. So we adjust the facts for Sheriff Coleman's benefit."

"Meaning?"

"Stick to the basics, Dinah. You were dragged outside, injured, hysterical from what you'd gone through."

"Wait a second, now..."

Thorn forged ahead as if she hadn't spoken. "I was cut but followed you outside. I saw the crazy woman start to stab you, and I shot her. After that, I can't remember much of anything. Do you?"

Color had crept into her cheeks. "I sure as hell remember more than that. After you fired, she got picked up and—"

"Picked up by the cyclone," Thorn suggested.

"And I saw her torn in half, for God's sake! Could a cyclone on the plains do that?"

"They flatten houses, barns, whole towns sometimes," Thorn said. "I'd hate to guess what kind of damage one person would suffer, sucked up in the air like that."

"But, damn it, Gideon, we *saw*!"

"Saw what?" he challenged her. "A giant ghost? Some kind of god conjured from thin air by an ancient ritual? You try telling the sheriff that..."

"And he'll believe I've lost my mind. I know. Goddamn it!"

"And something else," he said.

"Which is?"

"You go on record with a story, and you have to stick with it. No change of heart a week or month from now, trying to run another version in the *Sentinel*."

"The people have a right to know, don't they?"

"Know what, exactly? Your responsibility, as I'm given to understand it, is reporting news."

"Exactly! And—"

"Sagrado's had eight murders, counting Marshal Pike. Or maybe ten, if anyone can prove the Albrights were eliminated, so the cult could have their farm. All of the ones responsible are dead now, lying stacked up at the undertaker's shop."

"Or *sacked* up," Dinah interjected, "if we count the woman. What was left of her, I mean."

"Storm damage," Thorn repeated, "and coyotes get some of the credit too, I wouldn't be surprised."

He thought about their frantic exit from the farm, riding on Shadow and the marshal's brindle gelding, Charley Kuhn tied to his chestnut mare as well as they could manage, without doing him more injury. Elmo Dickson and some others had retrieved the rest, their bodies heaped up in his wagon, and Dinah was right. What they'd recovered of the woman fit inside a burlap bag.

"It isn't right to lie," she said. Thorn heard surrender in her voice.

"Consider the alternative," he answered, as they reached her office. "You could terrify your fellow townspeople—the ones who might believe you, anyway—and what then? Do they pull up stakes and leave, fearing a repetition of the murders and whatever else you sell them on?"

"They should be warned!"

"You heard the shaman, Dinah. He had one shot in a thousand years, and it fell through. Nobody here, or anywhere on Earth, will be alive the next time stars align, or whatever it was. And *that's* assuming there are any Mayans left, after last night."

"You think those were the last of them?"

"I'm damned if I know, but it won't be preying on my mind," Thorn said.

JUNE 10-11, 1876

Thorn stayed in town for Orrin Pike's funeral, on the Saturday. Before that, Sheriff Coleman came and went, asking his questions, getting nothing out of stitched-up Charley Kuhn, viewing the Mayan bodies at the undertaker's parlor. He was scowling when he left, but seemed inclined to let the matter lie—perhaps, Gideon thought, already planning how he'd spin it out, to make himself the hero of the story for his next election bid.

On Sunday, Thorn slept in while most of those remaining in Sagrado and environs went to church, hoping that Reverend Alonzo Jefferson could make some sense out of the nightmare they'd been living through and had, somehow, survived. Walking across the street for a late breakfast at McGuffy's restaurant, he saw them exiting the Free Will Church of God, most of their faces etched in varied shades of disappointment.

That made sense, Thorn realized, since there was nothing in their Bible about Mayans or their Lord Kisin, much less men dressed like parrots, staging human sacrifices in the modern age. Thorn guessed that Reverend Jefferson had tied it in to Satan somehow, tossing out some lines from scripture as he tried to prove his case, and wound up settling nothing much of anything for anybody in his anxious congregation.

Which, in Thorn's experience, was just about the way of things at Sunday morning services, no matter what a given preacher called his church or how he phrased his prayers to the Invisible Almighty somewhere up above. Thorn's restless wanderings included many stops at houses pledged to

"God" in one form or another, and he'd never seen a minister, regardless of his title or denomination, who'd seemed more concerned with answers than with passing the collection plate.

A waitress whom Thorn hadn't seen before greeted him, welcomed him to McGuffy's as if it was his first visit, and conveyed him to a window seat, though not the one he'd grown accustomed to. It hardly mattered, watching as the Sunday supplicants passed by, a handful stopping in to dine, most heading for their homes.

Thorn ordered scrambled eggs, biscuits and gravy, fried potatoes on the side, and waited while the waitress filled his coffee cup. A moment later, while he sipped the hot, black brew, he spotted Dinah Pilcher headed his way, not coming from church, but from the general direction of her office at the *Sentinel*. She ducked into the restaurant, addressed the waitress by her first name, then pointed to Thorn and mouthed something that looked like "I'm with him."

When she was seated opposite and had her order taken —two fried eggs, with toast, coffee in front of her—she said, "I'm guessing you skipped church this morning."

Nodding, Thorn replied, "I didn't think the reverend would add much to what we already know."

She tried her coffee, set the mug back down, and said, "The trouble is, I'm not sure *what* I know. I mean, we saw the same things, more or less, but how in hell do I report it to the town? If I keep lying to them, what good am I as a journalist?"

"Or," Thorn suggested, "you could ask yourself what good you'd do telling the truth, as we observed it. Who'd believe it, for a start? The quickest way to wreck your reputation is to peddle what your readers will dismiss as fantasy. At best, they'll think you were hysterical and haven't cleared your head yet. And at worst..."

"They'll think I've gone stark raving crazy. Right." She made a sour face. "So I keep lying, try to make them comfortable, not cause them to worry about what might come for them tomorrow, or the next day, or next year."

"What's wrong with that?" Thorn asked her.

"Seriously?"

Thorn leaned toward her, lowering his voice. "I'm absolutely serious. The fact is, you don't know whatever might be coming from them next week, or next year, but it's a safe bet that it won't be Mayans snatching hearts. Remember that they have to wait another thousand years, at least."

"I guess that lets me off the hook, then, doesn't it? I just grind out a vague description of events and wind up telling them the danger's past, nothing to fear from here on out."

"They'll always have enough to fear," he said, "without a newspaper fanning the flames. Maybe a story with an ending is exactly what the townsfolk need right now."

"It feels like cheating. Keeping secrets."

"By which you mean it's hard on *you*. It's always hardest on the people keeping secrets, rather than the rest who go about their daily business, unconcerned."

"You know I studied journalism, right? And secret keeping isn't in the job description."

"So, you're learning as you go along."

She eyed him carefully, face softening, and said, "You keep your share of secrets, too, I think."

"And chances are I'll take them to my grave."

Their meals arrived, and Gideon was digging in before Dinah set down her fork and drew her handbag up into her lap. "This almost slipped my mind," she said, dipping a hand inside her purse. "It came for you, care of the *Sentinel.*"

Thorn took the envelope she passed across to him and recognized the stationery instantly, the penmanship that formed his name, the paper's title, and the rest of it.

"You see I haven't opened it," she said.

Thorn didn't check the seal, taking her word for it.

"I did read the return address, though," she continued. "Boston. May I ask about the sender's name? The 'O. Magoro' strikes me as unusual."

"It's African," Thorn told her. "First name's 'Obi.' He's been with my family a long time, and helped raise me while my Aunt Drusilla dealt with other things."

"And even here, he's tracked you down." She poised to take a bite of toast, saying, "Please read it, if you like. I promise not to question you."

"No hurry," Thorn said. "It'll keep." He slipped the envelope into an inside pocket of his frock coat.

Dinah switched directions, saying, "You'll be leaving soon, I guess."

"This afternoon, in fact."

"As soon as that?" Thorn heard a hint of disappointment in her voice, but didn't bite. "Your people know I came here to investigate the murders. Now they've stopped, they'll soon be tired of me and wondering what's coming next, if I don't go."

"You say that like you've been through it before."

"Most everywhere I go," Thorn said.

"That strikes me as a lonely kind of life."

"Depends on what you're used to, I suppose."

"It makes me sad that you've grown used to it."

"No need to feel that way on my account, Dinah. I'll

have another job before you know it, and it's off to somewhere new."

"That satisfies you, does it?"

"Finding answers satisfies me, to a point."

"And after that?"

He shrugged. "More questions. Hopefully, more answers."

"But they're not the one you're really looking for."

His parents, right. "My guess would be, that ship has sailed," he said.

They finished up in silence, and the waitress came to take away their plates. Thorn paid, dismissing Dinah's offer that they split the bill. Outside, she said, "I never thanked you properly, did I?"

"For what?"

"Saving my life that night."

He smiled and said, "Well, I was in the neighborhood, and—"

Dinah hushed him with a kiss, hard on the lips, right there in broad daylight and never mind who might be watching. When she pulled away at last, blushing, she said, "I won't ask if you'll ever pass this way again. Why would you, anyhow?"

"You never know," he said, and knew how lame it sounded, even as he spoke.

"Good-bye, Gideon Thorn."

He watched her go, until she ducked into her office, then withdrew the envelope she'd handed him. Tearing it open, he skimmed Obi's brief handwritten note, then palmed the telegram folded within, posted from Dillon, in the Colorado Territory. Reading it, he felt a chill worm down his spine.

"Mr. Thorn, you don't know me but it's happening again. Stop."

A LOOK AT HALLOWED GROUND (GIDEON THORN BOOK 6)

BY MICHAEL NEWTON

Some wounds never heal. Some monsters never die.

On the eve of Colorado's statehood, Gideon Thorn follows a trail of blood back to where it all began. Decades ago, when he was just two years old, a savage beast—dismissed by some as a grizzly bear—tore through his family's homestead, leaving his parents and older brother butchered and Thorn himself marked by a white-streaked scar that never let him forget.

Now, settlers are vanishing again. Families wiped out. Bodies devoured. Something has returned to the high country, and Thorn can no longer avoid the place where his life was shattered.

Joined by his steadfast mentor Obi Magoro and intrepid newswoman Dinah Pilcher, Thorn must confront the nightmare that birthed his quest for truth—and find out whether the creature that shaped him is just a memory...or a living nightmare waiting in the pines.

AVAILABLE FEBRUARY 2026

ABOUT THE AUTHOR

A California native, Michael Newton published over 215 books under his own name and various pseudonyms since 1977. He began writing professionally as a "ghost" for author Don Pendleton on the best-selling Executioner series. With 104 episodes published to date, Newton nearly tripled the number of Mack Bolan novels completed by creator Pendleton himself.

www.ingramcontent.com/pod-product-compliance
Lightning Source LLC
LaVergne TN
LVHW040219110826
845146LV00005B/1344

* 9 7 9 8 8 9 5 6 7 9 0 9 8 *